FU

BODIED

A Francine Witt Mystery

Steve Exeter

First Edition

ISBN: 9798329162943

For the original

Terry and Dick

Contents

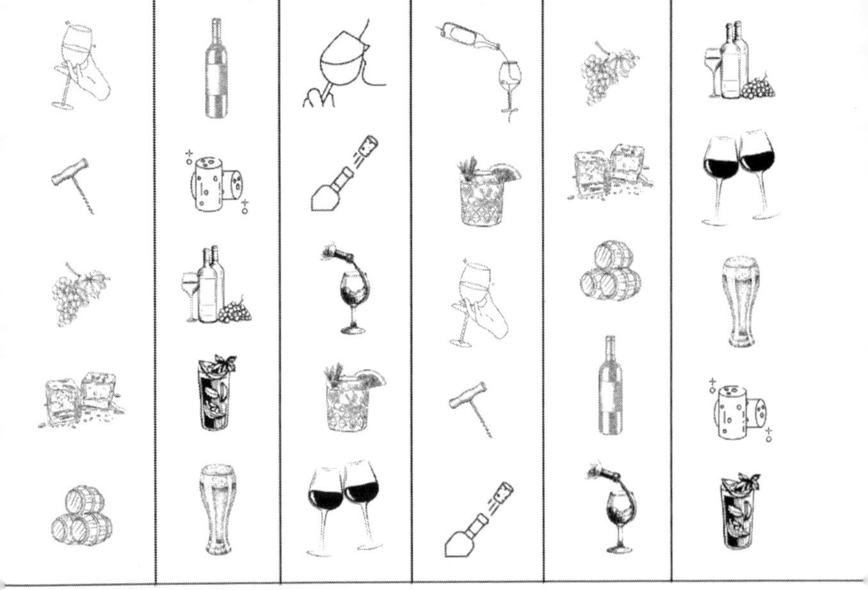

Pinot & Playhouses

A Heist-y Exit

Welcome back to Pinot & Playhouses where we make wine and theatre accessible to the masses. Today, we're at it again talking about the notorious boys about town who simply must have expensive bottles of wine, despite not having the inclination to pay for it. In the latest instalment of A Heist-y Exit, the boys managed to pilfer not one, but two bottles of Montrachet (a very expensive dry white wine, for those of you wondering) from the beautiful Café Jardin.

How? You ask.

Well, this time around they employed a different ruse. After ordering the first bottle of the Montrachet, which the waiter poured for them, the boys then ordered their meals, with one ordering the lobster bisque and the other ordering the risotto. Only seconds after the food was placed before them (on an immaculately white tablecloth) one of the boys (the risotto-eater) began choking. A waiter heroically performed the Heimlich manoeuvre, saving the choking man. A pound coin, ladies and gentlemen. That's what our antagonist was choking on. In a fluster, the maître d' apologised to the men offering them a bottle of champagne, as an olive branch. The boys refused, stating that they didn't drink champagne (who doesn't drink champagne?) In lieu of champagne, they were instead offered another bottle of Montrachet, which they quickly accepted before hightailing for the door. It wasn't until after the boys had left with two bottles of wine in hand, and their bill unpaid, that the waitstaff put two-and-two together. When one of the waiters (a fan of Pinot & Playhouses) shared my previous accounts of the boys' tea-leafing antics with his colleagues, they realised they'd been the latest victim in a string of wine heists. By my count, this is the fifth wine heist that we're aware of, and who knows how many others have gone under the radar. The question remains… is it worth it? What's wrong with a ten pound bottle of pinot grigio from Tesco? For many of us, Montrachet is way out of budget, and we get along just fine with a bottle of wine from our local supermarket. What makes these boys different from the rest of us?

Let me know what you think in the comments. Like, share, and follow Pinot & Playhouses for the latest news and tips in wine and theatre.

Cheers!

Francine Witt (the woman behind Pinot & Playhouses)

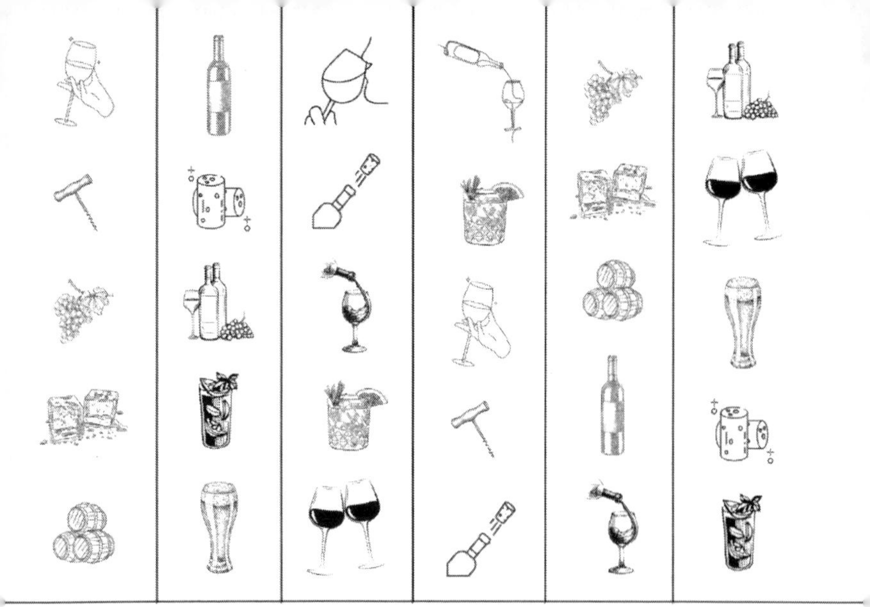

Wine Time

The camera lenses stare at me, wide-eyed and hungry. My eyes ache from preventing myself from rolling them live on air. I cringe at my own words, but I can't let the audience of middle-aged women desperate to know the latest wine news see that. Today, on my weekly segment of daytime TV (WINE TIME), I'm letting them in on the secrets of how to find the best budget bottle of wine. We're in the middle of an economic crisis, after all, and people rely on wine to get them through it, myself included. It's not exactly top-tier reporting, but I've got to afford wine (and my flat in a recently gentrified area of London) somehow. I give them the lowdown… A merlot from Morrisons. A chardonnay from Sainsbury's. A pinot grigio from… Lidl. The audience eats it up, they always do. I'm not exactly big news, but the sales of the wines I mention on *Wake-Up & Shake-Up* (the UK's leading weekday morning show) skyrocket every time without fail. I'm good at my job. It's not exactly how I saw my top-notch journalism degree being put to use, but I'm a semi-household name, so…

'Thank you, Francine,' the chirpy, bleach-blonde presenter, Marigold, says. 'I know what I'll be adding to my shopping list this week.' We all know that she doesn't have to buy budget wine, but I smile anyway. Marigold is likeable, and successful, and I'm probably just jealous.

'You're welcome,' I reply, walking off the stage.

'Up next, the Egyptologists behind QUEEN NEFERTITI: THE ROYAL TOUR join us to tell us all about their exciting exhibition at the British Museum. Talk about girl power, right Max?' she says to the greying co-host who looks like he'd rather poke his eyes out with his Parker pen than talk about girl power.

'Yes, Marigold, very exciting.'

They cut to an ad break as a gaggle of suit-wearing nerds walk into the room. I mean 'nerds' as a term of endearment, of course. Anybody still in academia past their thirties, which these people clearly are, are quite obviously nerds. There are five of them in total. Two women and three men. It's obvious that they're used to public speaking, they all look more than comfortable on *the couch.* After my segment, I usually run straight home to work on my blog or research for next week's segment, but something about the Egyptologists, this mismatched group of people, draws me to them. I grab myself a bitter coffee from the vending machine in the corner of the room and hang back to watch.

'Welcome back,' Max says, his smile not reaching his eyes. 'We are here with the world-renowned Egyptologists to discuss bringing Queen Nefertiti to the people of London. Throughout the next month, various activities and events will take place at the British Museum to commemorate the life of Queen Nefertiti, the great royal wife of Pharaoh Akhenaten.'

'Hermione Radcliffe, head of classical studies at the University of London,' Marigold says, turning her attention to the older of the two women. She gives off the air of a person who is to be respected, which immediately warms me to her. She's teetering on her later years. If I had to guess her age, I'd say she's in her early sixties. 'You are partially responsible for organising the exhibition, alongside your colleagues. What first sparked your interest with Queen Nefertiti?'

'It is impossible to overstate the impact that Queen Nefertiti has had upon modern society. She is a rarity in classical studies. She ruled side-by-side with her husband, Pharaoh Akhenaten, not a wallflower, but a co-monarch with full executive power.'

'So, it wasn't your grandfather's involvement in the excavation of the Valley of the Kings, and subsequent discovery of many of the artefacts that are on display in the exhibition today? Or your mother, Penelope Radcliffe, who was very involved in the search for Nefertiti's burial chamber in the 50s?' Max says, a smile pulling at his lips.

'Of course. Archaeology runs in my family. My grandfather, The Earl of Cadogan, George Walker, funded many of the excavations in the early 1900s. My mother, the subsequent Lady of Cadogan, continued his work. She was the first female archaeologist to lead a major dig in the country. This is something of which I am particularly proud. It was an exceedingly difficult time for a woman, particularly an unwed woman, to be in Egypt alone at that time, but my mother was very headstrong and independent. Due to my upbringing, I have always been fascinated with the classics. During my academic study, I found myself specialising in Queen Nefertiti, partially because of my mother's influence. Nefertiti was such a fascinating character, a feminist icon, and there is still so much we have left to learn about her. As her burial chamber, and therefore her mummified remains have never been found, at least that we can definitively prove, there are still many mysteries left to be solved. I do not know about you, but I find that fascinating.'

I smile inwardly, silently congratulating Hermione for her well-constructed response.

'There has been some contention regarding the ownership of the artefacts on display, has there not, Professor Hinksley?'

'The contention lies in the nature of the excavation and extraction of the artefacts. We live in a quite different time, and there is no denying that the collection of Egyptian artefacts amounted to gung-ho white imperialism. However, the priority for myself, and many other hardworking historians who collaborate with me at the Metropolitan Museum in New York, is to ensure that these incredible historical artefacts are shared with as many people as possible. Their value lies not only in providing invaluable insight into the ancient ways of life, but also in teaching and establishing a love of history and learning in future generations,' Professor Hinksley says, pushing his frameless glasses up his nose.

'Farouk Al Mohammad, you look like you have something to say? 'Marigold turns her attention to a gentleman dressed in a white linen suit, a marked contrast to his dark skin.

'The Egyptian Heritage Foundation and I believe that the *excavation* amounted to theft. The artefacts belonged to the Egyptian people. Many archaeologists at this time were nothing more than thieves. They, along with the rest of their party, consistently ignored the terms of their excavation visas. Not only that, but their carelessness led to valuable treasures being lost, which amounts to a crime in itself. Around the time of Penelope Radcliffe's last excavation, Egypt was facing a time of revolution and a newfound nationalism. The Egyptian government consequently took control of their archaeological institutions, including its four main museums, with the aim that they could reinstate the autonomy over their own nation. This included their artefacts and any areas of archaeological significance. Essentially, Egypt was taking ownership of their history and their future, instead of allowing rich white men to control them.'

'Hermione, do you have a response to that?' Max says, looking pointedly at Hermione.

'As I previously said, it was very much a different time back then. We have progressed significantly in terms of how we construct archaeological digs nowadays. Do I agree with the way my grandfather constructed his digs? Absolutely not. We have learned a lot since then, and it's time we moved on. My mother is a slightly different story. She is not a rich white man, but she is a rich white woman. However, it must be acknowledged that Egypt was a dangerous place for a white woman to be, especially as the revolution was beginning to peak its head. Wherever possible, my mother tried to be inclusive and empathetic to the Egyptian people. Her only aim was to find out what happened to Nefertiti. Unfortunately, her final dig was a failure. She found nothing of particular historical relevance, other than the Amarna amulet, of course. That being said, she paved the way for females in this field, like Gillian and I. And I feel proud to be a female face in such a male dominated field.

'In the exhibition we have artefacts from many different collections for the public to enjoy. It really is an extremely exciting time in classics circles, and I'm thrilled to be part of the team bringing Queen Nefertiti to the people of London.'

'May I?' the *other* woman interjects, politely.

'Of course, Gillian Cox,' Max says, giving his best puppy-dog expression. I resist the urge to roll my eyes at how differently he speaks to the more traditionally attractive of the two women.

'As a woman in the twenty-first century, part of the magic of the exhibition lies in the femininity of Queen Nefertiti, the *female pharaoh,* if you will. Independent of how the artefacts came to light, the fact is that they did, which we should all be entirely grateful for as it shed light on something still unfathomable to many people in today's society... A female ruler. And this was thousands of years ago. If that doesn't inspire young girls, then I don't know what will.'

'Your latest book, *The Female Pharaoh,* details a feminist take on Queen Nefertiti and is available in all good bookstores?' Marigold says, nodding eagerly at Gillian.

'Yes, it is, thank you.' The sincerity in Gillian's voice catches me off guard, she's created something she's immensely proud of.

'Doctor Van Bussell, what's your take on the exhibition?' Max says, practically ignoring Gillian's answer completely.

'Martin, please,' Doctor Van Bussell says. 'I agree with Hermione and Gillian. And might I also recommend Gillian's book? It is very well-researched but is also very accessible. It's a great read.' I'm sure I'm not the only one who notices that he places a hand on Hermione's knee for a second as he speaks. 'But back to the exhibition. Many of the artefacts have never been displayed before, or have only had limited interaction with the public. We have the bust of Nefertiti from the Fitzroy collection, the Amarna amulet, courtesy of Professor Hinksley,' Van Bussell gives a small nod to Hinksley across the sofa. 'We also have Nefertiti's papyrus slippers, which we have Farouk's government to thank for. This is truly a one-of-a-kind exhibition and is one not to be missed.'

As Max launches into a reel of information about how to buy tickets for the special events at the exhibit, I find my eyes drawn back to Hermione's neck where a deep purple stone sits at the end of a gold chain. It's huge, and gaudy, and in direct opposition to the rest of her demure outfit. The academics always seem to struggle with fashion. I might not have her success or respect, but I suppose at least I have a sense of style. At this point in my career, I'll take that as a win.

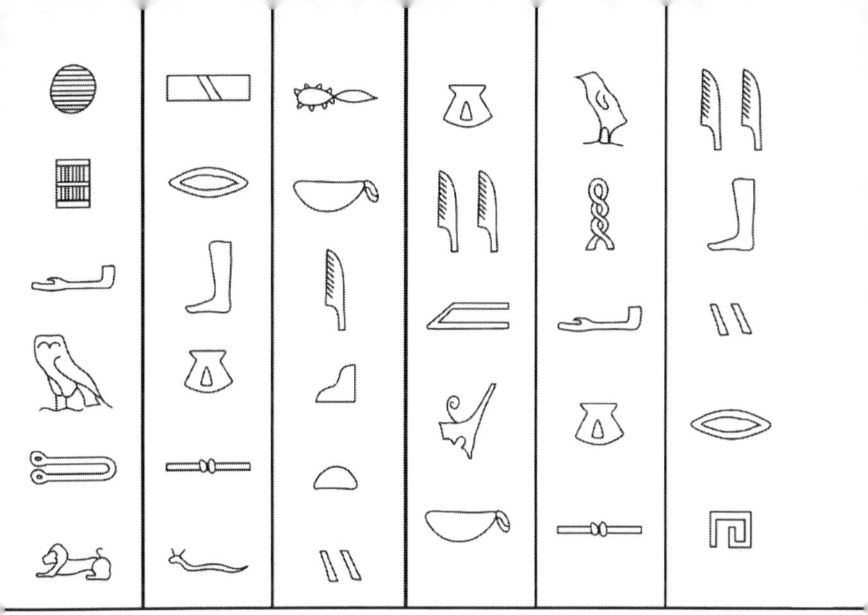

One Down

Ten bottles of open merlot stare at me from across the table. Each one cost between three and six pounds. I've sipped and sipped for an hour and they're all starting to taste the same. Based on my research, these are the contenders for the 'best budget merlot'. The blog post is scheduled to be released next month, but I like to work a few weeks in advance just in case something more exciting crops up. It never does. I listen to the news while I work, a habit I picked up back at uni. You can't be a serious journalist and not know what's going on in the world, and so the news is my constant background noise whatever I'm doing. It's driven my previous boyfriends insane. 'Why can't you listen to music like a normal person?' the last one said, as though my habit of listening to the news was as bad as his habit of leaving wet towels on the bed or flicking toenail clippings all across the laminate floor. I half-laugh at the memory, shaking my head at how stupid I was to put up with his shit.

I turn back to the wine at hand, my mind reeling with flavour profiles and acidity. As much as I want to choose one at random and say it's the best, I can't. My audience deserves better than that. Although, recently, they haven't been engaging as much with the wine review content as they have with the wine heists. There's just something about your average Joe stealing expensive bottles of wine from expensive restaurants that the public likes. They LOVE an anti-hero, especially in the form of two bumbling young men turned Robin Hood figures. Talk about serious reporting. Whenever a maître d or waiter calls or emails me with the latest details of another wine heist, I jump. I'm gaining followers faster than I can keep up thanks to those blog posts. I've sold my soul to the devil, but it pays the bills.

'You join us live from outside the British Museum where reporter Hayden James has updates following the breaking news of the death of Professor Abu Hinksley, of the Metropolitan Museum in New York.'

I squint at the TV, taking the reading glasses from my face.

'The incident occurred less than half an hour ago, at the commencement speech of the QUEEN NEFERTITI: THE ROYAL TOUR exhibit.' Hayden James speaks directly into the camera. His face the perfect mask of solemnity. 'Professor Abu Hinksley stood at the podium and began to give his speech when he collapsed on stage. Paramedics arrived in minutes. By this time, a doctor in the audience had already pronounced Professor Hinksley to be dead at the scene, after performing CPR. The death is being treated as suspicious, as you can see from the police presence around the museum.'

The camera pans outwards so that the audience can see the police presence.

'One of the members of the audience told me that she saw Professor Hinksley drinking out of a water glass, with a slice of lemon, in the seconds prior to his collapse. It has been suggested that his drink may have been poisoned.'

I almost turn the TV off at his shoddy reporting. It is unethical to cast aspersions so soon after the death of a public figure, especially when you have nothing but petty gossip to support your claims. Hayden's words become white noise as I focus on the commotion happening behind him. Other reporters are clamouring forward towards a middle-aged gentleman in a crumpled suit. Hayden, predictably, doesn't notice the other reporters and carries on talking shit into the camera. I mute the TV and turn to the internet as a source of information.

The facts, as far as I can ascertain, are as follows:

1. Professor Abu Hinksley (48 years old) died on stage in front of a room full of expectant faces.
2. He was a tenured professor at the MET museum in New York and was very respected amongst other academics.
3. He was an outspoken believer that Nefertiti was black (and apparently this is the cause of much contention amongst historians).
4. Just prior to his death, he did take a sip of water. (I roll my eyes as I read this.)
5. The exhibition is closed for the rest of the evening, and possibly tomorrow, while the crime scene investigators do their thing.
6. Detective Wicks, the man that Hayden didn't see, gave a comment that the police are treating the death as suspicious and if the public has any information, they should come forward.

Death is always a bizarre notion to face. Yesterday morning, I'd watched the professor talk animatedly about the exhibit, and now he was dead. In all likelihood, he was laid on an autopsy table being scoured for clues. It's impossible not to acknowledge the fragility of life when you're faced with the prospect of death. At least Professor Hinksley lived a life that people will celebrate. He made drastic strides in archaeology, particularly Egyptology, and his name will be remembered by students and academics for years to come. That seems like a pretty nice legacy, if you ask me.

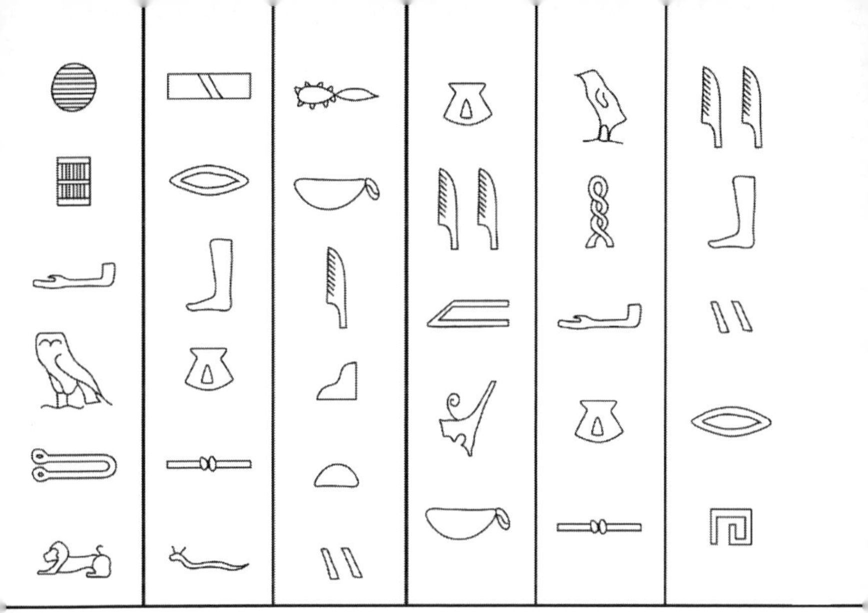

The Daily Vine: The Internet's Premier News Agency

Death of an Egyptologist

Death is not an uncommon topic in classical studies. After all, all of the subjects are long since dead. However, the death of an Egyptologist, opening an exhibition to celebrate the reign of Queen Nefertiti, that's less common. Yesterday, Professor Abu Hinksley, died on stage as he officially opened the QUEEN NEFERTITI: THE ROYAL

TOUR exhibit. In a statement released this morning, Detective Wicks, lead investigator in the case, has released the cause of death to the public.

'Results of the toxicology report state that the cause of death was poison. While we don't wish to release further details at this time, we want to reassure the public that they are not in any danger, and this appears to be an isolated attack.'

The exhibition will be reopened from 1.30 pm and is once again open to the public. Co-organiser, Hermione Radcliffe of the University of London, issued this statement: 'We are greatly saddened by the passing of our friend and colleague Abu Hinksley. Professor Hinksley was not only a respected voice amongst academics, but he was also a kind and loving friend. There was no doubt in our minds that we should keep the exhibit open in his honour. Abu worked so hard to bring the QUEEN NEFERTITI: THE ROYAL TOUR together, that it would be a great disservice to him to close it for any longer than necessary. We look forward to welcoming you all back to the exhibit, and hope that you see it as a celebration of both Nefertiti and Abu.'

For further details regarding the exhibit…

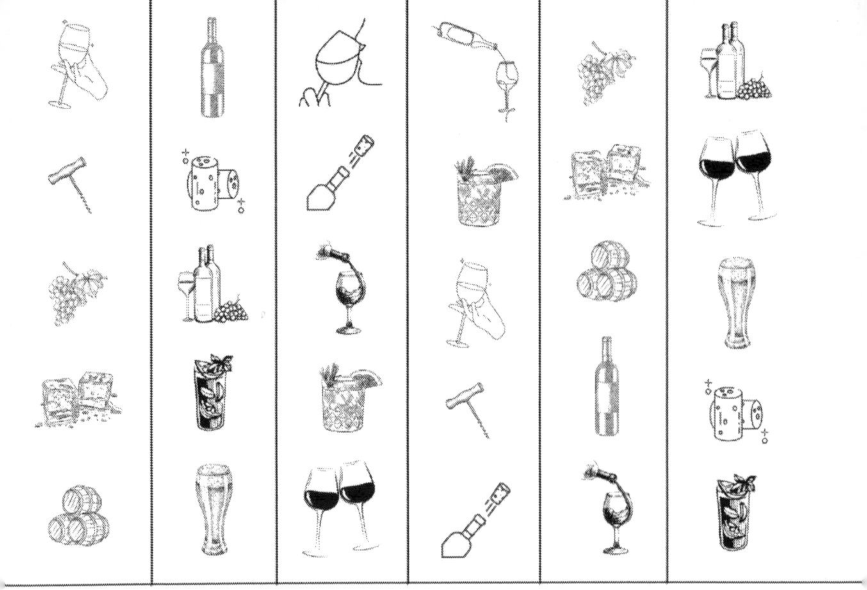

Not A Cougar

The phone call is a welcome distraction from my laptop. I've spent the day so far dealing with admin stuff and I'm bored out of my mind. It's a waiter from a local restaurant overlooking the Thames. There's been another heist. My name is currently whispered in restaurants around London, my email address and work phone number have spread like wildfire, just in case a restaurant gets hit by the infamous wine thieves. At least this way they get a bit of publicity out of the experience.

The restaurant, Waterside, is full to the brim when I get there. The typically unpredictable British weather has provided us with some sunshine, and when us Brits see the sun, we need to be near water, it's ingrained in us. Where better to go than a restaurant overlooking the, slightly murky, Thames? It's the kind of place that's perfect for a date, especially if you're dating in professional spheres. It's pricey, beautiful, and has a wine menu to die for, which is likely why the boys chose it.

Just outside, the waiter who called me, holds up his hand, stubbing out his cigarette on the stone building.

'Thanks for coming,' he says, reaching out to shake my hand.

'Thanks for the tip,' I say, and follow him inside. We head through the restaurant and onto the patio at the back. We sit at a table for two by the glass barrier. I peer over the edge, the lazy river below.

'Can I get you a drink?' he asks. His eyes bore into me. It's clear he wants me to accept the offer. He's young, very young. Maybe twenty, at a push. I'm a lot of things, but I'm not a cougar. Ten years ago, okay, five years ago, he'd have definitely been my type. Tall, dark, handsome, kind of like a young Patrick Swayze, pre-*Dirty Dancing.* I need somebody who's my age, with a job, and who is ready for commitment. My biological clock is ticking and if I want to become the Instagram-worthy working mum before I'm forty, I need to get a move on. Young Patrick Swayze over here isn't going to tick those boxes for me.

'No thanks. I've got a busy day ahead of me.' I hope he picks up on my cue, without me seeming impolite. I have a list of jobs as long as my arm, which I abandoned at the drop of a hat, and once I've got the details of the wine heist, I need to go and write it up and then get back to my list.

'Okay, no problem. So, do you just want me to tell you the story?'

'Yes, please. I'll record you on my phone if that's okay?' I place my phone on the table and press the record button. The waiter nods, and launches into his story.

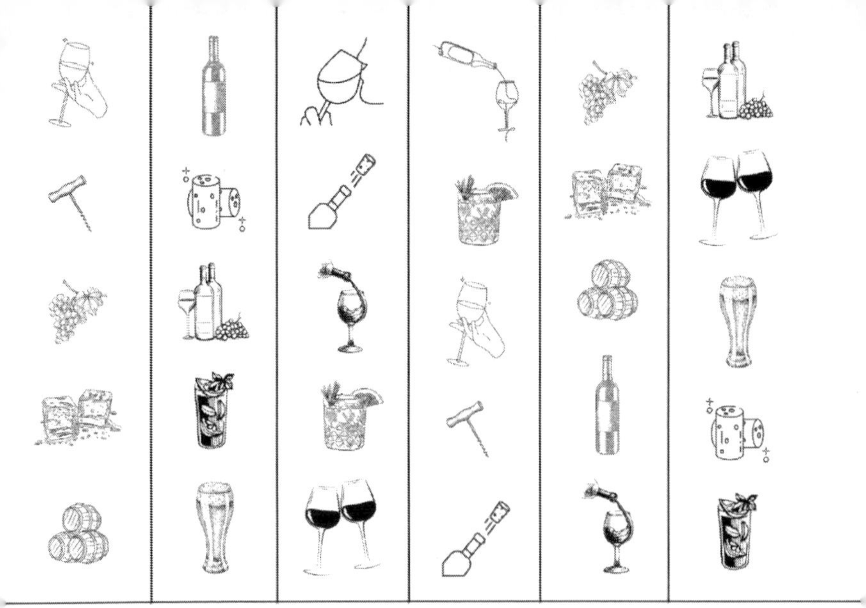

Pinot & Playhouses

Making a Splash

Welcome back to Pinot & Playhouses where we make wine and theatre accessible to the masses. I'll give you one guess who we're going to talk about… The boys are back. For those of you who are new here, let me recap. The boys, as they've affectionately become known through this blog series, are two young men who simply must have expensive wine that they apparently can't afford. So, do they read my blog and buy the best budget wine? Nope, they steal the expensive stuff. Today's wine heist was a fairly unusual one, I'll give them that.

Picture this... You're sitting on the outdoor terrace at the Waterside restaurant. The sun is shining and there's not a cloud in the sky. The weather is hot, and the wine is cold. You're with your friend (boyfriend? Brother? – at this point, we still don't know the nature of their relationship, so don't want to assume) sipping champagne and having a lovely time. At some point, you decide that the champagne isn't cutting it for you, and so you order a bottle of the Muscadet Sur Lie. The waiter arrives with the bottle and pours the beautiful crisp white wine into your glasses. The waiter leaves, you take a sip and enjoy the sparkling grassy taste. When the waiter leaves, you either (somehow?!) return the wine from your glasses to the bottle. Or, you drink up and re-cork the bottle (maybe you bring one of the plastic ones with you from home). And then, to get out of paying for your drinks, you jump over the glass railing and into a passing Thames Tour boat full of people.

Yes, ladies and gentlemen, you read that right. A TOUR BOAT FULL OF PEOPLE. An accident waiting to happen, you might say. And yes, the boys' reckless actions, while comical (if you like slapstick) did injure the boat's tour guide who found himself assaulted by one of the falling bodies. The other falling body, somehow, managed to miss the boat completely and land straight in the Thames.

After a few moments of confusion, the two boys meet up on dry land when the boat docked on a nearby jetty. The flabbergasted tourists watched as the boys legged it down the street, only to be confronted by two heroic waiters from the restaurant they'd just burgled. It has been suggested that the boys may be part feline as they managed to escape the waiters and disappear into the crowded streets, making their escape.

It is unknown whether they succeeded in keeping the bottle of Muscadet Sur Lie intact. For their sake, I hope they didn't waste such a delicious wine. So, dear reader, where do you think they'll hit next? Is nowhere safe from such villainous acts? Oh, I'm being a little sarcastic, but the point is valid. Why do these men think they're entitled to take wine (a luxury item) and not pay for it? What sets them apart from the rest of us? Are they really Robin Hood-esque heroes, or are they simply petty criminals?

Let me know what you think in the comments. Like, share, and follow Pinot & Playhouses for the latest news and tips in wine and theatre.

Cheers!

Francine (the woman behind Pinot & Playhouses)

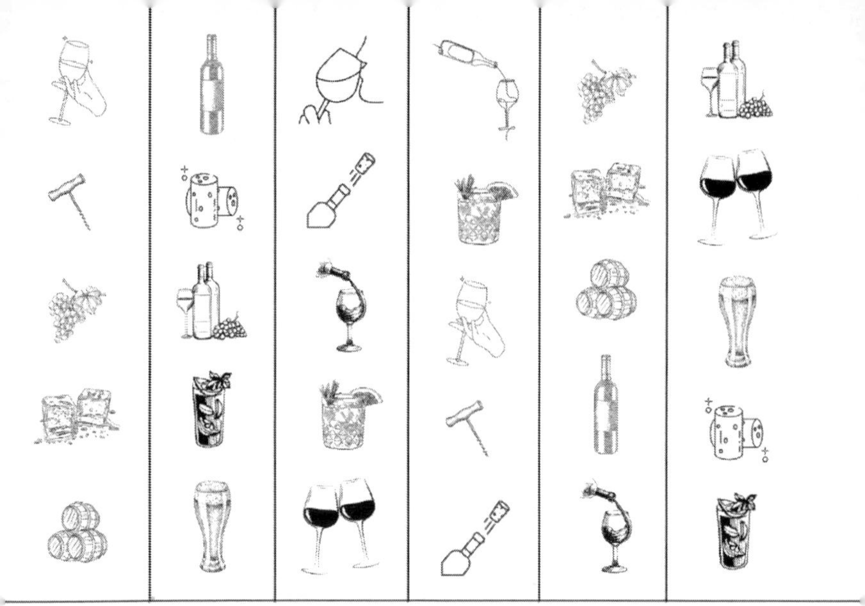

An Evening to Remember

As suspected, the latest blog post blew up. The public really does love hearing about the wine heists. I can't for the life of me think why. I sit and watch the numbers rise. The likes, shares, and comments. *This* is my legacy. *This* is what is going to be mentioned in my obituary. The advertising deals, the sponsorships, the freebies, are all becoming like nothing I ever imagined. These boys are making me famous. Of course, there's my weekly segment on daytime TV, and people in wine and theatre circles know who I am, but since I started writing about the wine heists, Pinot & Playhouses has gained so much traction. The readership has doubled in the last two weeks alone. I should be happy, I know that. And, believe me, I'm grateful for the freedom this provides me. Advertising deals and lucrative sponsorships are the only reason I can afford to rent my flat. Without them, I'd be off in the suburbs somewhere and I'd have no choice but to spend an hour on the train just to get to London. Right now, I'm in the heart of it. The suburbs will come later. I'd always considered there to be a before and after in my life. There would be the before success – where I'd work my arse off to be recognised, and the after success, where I lived in the suburbs with my beautiful husband, 2.5 kids, and a dog (preferably a lovely little Staffy, or something, but I'm not picky about that aspect). I'm concerned now that *this* is my successful period. This is my career peak. Not serious journalism, the stuff you win prizes for, writing about sex trafficking or corrupt politicians. No, I'm writing a blog about wine, the theatre, and two boys who think they're entitled to free wine.

Today is the day I make a change. Sort of. Today is a big day in the wine calendar. One that has been on my radar for a few months. My manager/agent, Keith, managed to snag me tickets to cover the biggest wine auction of the year… and all for a single bottle of Margaux. A 1943 Grand Vin Du Château Margaux magnum bottle, to be exact.

The Ivy is gorgeous. Objectively so. Ivy drapes over the walls, inside and out. There's warm uplighting which makes the room glow, and candles adorn every table so that the restaurant flickers like it's on fire. Unfortunately, Keith has decided to act as my chaperone for the evening. Any excuse to drink expensive wine and irritate the hell out of me. As much as Keith annoys me, he's indispensable as far as my career is concerned. He's the one that wangled the *Wake Up* gig, so I have to put up with him.

We're shown to our table by a waiter dressed all in black, a single ivy leaf decorates the pocket of his dress shirt. As we sit, the waiter hands Keith the wine menu and I try not to openly cringe. Keith, bless his misogynistic little heart, pretends to look it over before handing it to me and saying, 'I'll let you choose this evening, darling.'

The waiter nods his head and stands with hands behind his back. I take my time, making sure that the waiter knows I know what I'm talking about. Most people in attendance this evening do. It *is* a wine auction, after all. I order a bottle of the chardonnay for Keith and I to share, and he nods at me like he agrees with my choice. Together, we sit back and watch the semi-famous faces of almost celebrities, like myself, pile into the room. As coincidence would have it, Prunella Downing, star of the stage, is shown to her table. I have an interview booked in with her in the next couple of days, thanks to my pestering Keith to get me some more serious gigs. Prunella is well-respected in the classical theatre scene; a world-renowned Shakespearian actor who only does plays that people pretend to understand and like. I peer over the top of my chardonnay and watch Prunella chatting away to her daughter. They're both incredibly beautiful women, dainty and bird-like. They have the same slim features, and natural-looking auburn hair, although I doubt Prunella's is natural. I'm greying already and she has at least thirty years on me. I make a mental note to look up her age, and other background information I'd need to know before our interview. I want to be prepared.

Keith is engrossed in his phone, as always. I'm not his only client, but I am his biggest earner. The cut he takes from my wages often makes me question whether I could go it alone. A group of people walk into the restaurant, four in total, and I recognise them immediately as the Egyptologists. Small world. I glance back at Prunella, who rolls her eyes theatrically and stands, waving her hand in the direction of Hermione.

'My darling sister,' she calls across the restaurant, in a voice too posh to be her real accent.

'What are you doing here?' Hermione says, as Prunella pulls her into a hug.

'We're here for the auction, of course,' Prunella says.

'Rosalind, it's lovely to see you,' Hermione says.

Rosalind stands and hugs Hermione. Her aunt? Prunella had said, 'my darling sister'.

As much as I had no reason to connect Prunella and Hermione as sisters, their relationship takes me by surprise. They're total opposites.

'Hello Auntie Hem,' Rosalind says. 'What a pleasant surprise.'

Who talks like that? I think to myself.

'We're here for the auction too. I didn't think it was your kind of event.' The tone she takes towards Prunella verges on condescending.

'I love wine, and I love auctions,' Prunella says. The wide smile on her face reminds me of a Barbie doll, entirely fake; plastic.

'Would you like to sit together?' A waiter approaches and looks between the two women. They each pause for a moment, seemingly too polite to say no.

'That would be lovely, thank you,' Prunella says.

The waiter pulls the nearby table close to Prunella and Rosalind, and the Egyptologists take their seats.

'This is Farouk, Martin and Gillian,' Hermione says, gesturing to her colleagues. 'And this is my sister, Prunella, and my niece, Rosalind.'

There is an exchanging of pleasantries and a shaking of hands. I zone out as Prunella politely asks questions about the others, sipping my chardonnay. The waiter returns with the wine menu. They each order their own drinks, Farouk ordering tap water.

Thanks to Keith's obsession with his phone, I'm able to earwig on the Egyptologists. I don't know why I find them so fascinating, but I do.

'Do you intend to bid on the bottle?' Hermione asks her sister.

'I'm not sure yet. I haven't decided. Will you be bidding?'

If I had a sister, I don't believe for a second I'd speak to her in the stilted way these two siblings are talking. It's a forced politeness that makes me feel incredibly uncomfortable.

'Yes, I believe I will.'

I watch as Hermione and Van Bussell share a look that I can't quite decipher. A challenge?

'Why? Do you have more money than sense?' Prunella asks. It is worded in a way that suggests she's joking, but Hermione clearly prickles.

'No, I don't,' Hermione says. 'The wine is rumoured to have been smuggled back from Egypt around the time of the final coup when all of the archaeologists, including our mother, were banished from the country. As such, it holds a personal significance to me, as well as many other Egyptologists. I'm sure my friend, Martin, will also be bidding on it.'

Van Bussell gives a little nod in Prunella's direction. 'That I shall.'

Interesting. I'd heard rumours that the wine bottle had been engraved with some 'aftermarket' text or symbols, but the press hadn't yet released photographs. It was suggested that the engravings added to the value of the bottle, rather than detracted from it, which was rather unusual to say the least. Usually, if the bottle was marked in some way, the value plummeted.

As more people file in and take their seats, the conversation between the Egyptologists, and Prunella and her daughter, becomes blurred. I catch bits and pieces, but nothing of interest to me. When the room is finally filled, the auction begins.

A makeshift stage stands at the back end of the restaurant, and behind it, a projector screen has been erected. The screen flashes to life, the projector itself somewhere in the depths of the audience. A man who looks as old as time itself comes to stand before the room, behind a wooden lectern that looks completely out of place in the modern restaurant.

'Good evening, ladies and gentlemen, and welcome to this momentous occasion. We are here this evening to auction off a one-of-a-kind bottle of vintage Margaux. On the screen behind me, you'll see photographs of the bottle in question. There have been many aspersions cast about the nature of the engravings on the bottle. Today is the first time that these will be shown to the public. The bottle is being auctioned by Cutler and Sons, and is the only piece up for auction today.'

The projector screen is filled with a video of the bottle of wine. It starts with the bottle a distance away, a full-frontal shot, and then zooms in on the etchings. I cast a glance at the Egyptologists who have pulled pens and paper out of thin air. Their glances go between the screen and their notepads, their pens moving so fast that they blur.

'This wine is of significant historical value. The Margaux, particularly this vintage, was a popular drink amongst Europeans and Americans in Egypt during archaeological digs. This particular bottle was brought back to the UK sometime after the Egyptian revolution, which saw all archaeological digs conducted by foreign sources outlawed in the country. As you can see, the etchings are a particularly fascinating addition to the bottle. The source (and meaning) behind them is unknown, but rumour has it that they are the key to lost treasure.'

The auctioneer says the last part of the sentence like he doesn't believe a word of it, the same way one might talk about healing crystals or Scientology.

'To quote the literature behind the production of this fine vintage, "*This vintage was a tremendous success. It was the best wine produced at Château Margaux, and in Bordeaux generally, since 1934. We think back to those difficult times and conditions during the war with feelings of great sympathy. Many things were lacking: personnel, horses, spray products, generally everything. The success of this vintage is all the more touching. Château Margaux 1943 is perfect to drink now. Its bouquet is fine, elegant, closer to the great vintages of the 1950s, like 1953, than the other great wines produced in the 1940s. On the palate, it is tender and harmonious, finishing on a smooth rather than dry note. This delicious wine, to drink now, can still be kept for several more years without any problems.*" The historical significance, coupled with the fantastic vintage, makes this particular bottle incredibly desirable.'

The bidding begins and I quickly lose track of the numbers as they rise. This isn't an ordinary bottle of wine, it's a legacy piece. When it comes down to it, only two people are left in a vicious bidding war. Hermione and her colleague Martin Van Bussell.

When a man randomly interjects with his first bid of the evening, all eyes turn to him, including his companion. The bidding is already in the tens of thousands, and it isn't showing any signs of slowing down.

'What?' the man shrugs to his friend.

The friend rolls his eyes and says, 'Shut up, Terry. We can't afford it.' He waves his hand in the direction of the auctioneer, gesturing for him to continue. The crowd mumble something as a whole – likely, 'what the hell?' – and the auctioneer continues.

The tense, quick-fire bidding surmises with Hermione having been dealt the winning hand.

'Congratulations,' the auctioneer says, and the auction closes.

Hermione smiles as wide as the Cheshire cat. Moments later, a waiter appears at their table. 'Will you be drinking the wine this evening, or would you like it packaged to take home.'

It never crossed my mind that the winner of the auction would want to drink the wine the same evening, especially not when the bidding had gone as high as it had.

'Could you package it up and bring it to the table please?' Hermione says.

'Of course.' The waiter backs away and vanishes into the kitchen, presumably to wrap up the bottle of wine.

'Congratulations,' Van Bussell says to Hermione curtly.

'Thank you, Martin,' Hermione replies.

The tension is thick in the air between the two of them. I catch Gillian, the author, wink at Hermione.

'I assume that you'll be keeping the bottle to yourself and not sharing with your colleagues,' Martin says.

'For now, I'll be keeping the bottle private,' Hermione confirms.

Van Bussell remains poker-faced. He seemed to expect that response.

The bottle returns to the table wrapped in a grey giftbag with The Ivy logo printed on it. The waiter hands it to Hermione who places it on the floor in between her ankles. Van Bussell glances down and outwardly cringes. I can't blame him. It's an expensive bottle to put on the floor.

Two blokes approach the table. The ones with the random bid mid-auction.

'Congratulations,' the taller of the two says.

'Thank you,' Hermione replies curtly.

'I'm Dick, and this is my friend Terry.'

'Hermione,' Hermione says. Her smile doesn't reach her eyes.

'May I ask why you chose to bid so high on the wine?' Dick asks.

Terry stands by his side like a statue. His eyes are fixed on Rosalind.

'For exactly the reasons the auctioneer said. We're Egyptologists and this wine holds significant value for us, given its past.'

Dick's mouth opens comically wide. 'Wait, was one of your lot murdered yesterday?'

I bite my lip to keep me from laughing. Talk about subtlety.

The group nods solemnly.

'May we join you?' Dick asks.

There are looks of confusion between the Egyptologists (and Prunella and Rosalind) but, once again, British politeness takes precedence, and the men are invited to join the group.

Terry is immediately dragged into a conversation by Rosalind. He leans close, turning on the charm. Although I can't make out their words, their flirting is painfully obvious.

It is Hermione who keeps my attention. She is very clearly in a leadership position within her group. The others look to her regularly for encouragement, although they likely don't realise that's what they're doing. Van Bussell seems to be retaining most of Hermione's interest. They're locked in a disagreement about the race of Ancient Egyptians. As he speaks, Van Bussell bends close to her, their heads almost touching.

As it happens with groups of people, their conversations layer over one another until I can barely make out one voice from another. The drinks flow, the food comes and goes, and yet the Margaux remains untouched between Hermione's feet. Every so often, Dick and Terry make eye contact and shrug before going back to their own conversations. For the most part, Terry is practically drooling over Rosalind. It's always funny to watch people flirt. I sip my wine and try my best to pick out individual voices. I eventually give up, choosing to soak in the atmosphere instead.

'I meant to tell you, I've been talking to *Gossip & Gardens* about a monthly feature. They're really interested in you, and the pay is phenomenal. Just need to iron out some details.'

I'd all but forgotten Keith was there until he spoke.

'I thought we agreed that we'd stick to more serious jobs,' I say.

'Yes, but the money…' Keith says.

'Keith,' I shake my head. Every single time I ask for more serious proper journalistic jobs, he promises the world and delivers the exact opposite. 'I said I wasn't going to do that anymore. Daytime TV is one thing, writing for a shit magazine that only people bored out of their minds in hospital read, isn't what I had in mind. I won't do it.'

'You'll change your mind when you see the pay offer,' he grins.

'I won't.' I fold my arms over my chest and sigh. I turn my back to Keith and try to pretend he isn't there.

As ten o'clock rolls around, Dick and Terry stand as though cued by some invisible chime. The table goes silent and looks up to them.

'It's been lovely to meet you all, but it's time we headed home. We'll just nip and pay the bill and be off. Thank you for a lovely evening.'

As Dick speaks, all attention on him, Terry pulls the gift bag under the table and tucks it into a supermarket carrier bag. It clicks where I know them from. They're *the boys.* The wine thieves that caused my blog to blow up. One more coincidence to add to the list. I toy with the idea of informing Hermione that her pricey bottle of wine has been stolen. A better person might have told her, but it would blow my cover. As much as I went out tonight with the intention of being a serious reporter, I now have a front-row seat to a wine heist, and I have to pay my bills somehow. I will thank the boys for that, one day. I wonder if they're even aware of the blog post detailing their indiscretions.

Dick and Terry walk away. If I hadn't just seen them steal a (ridiculously) prestigious bottle of wine, I wouldn't have believed them capable of it. They look like two normal, if a little bit scruffy, blokes. They give a final wave to the table as they walk out of the door.

Prunella shoots a glance at Hermione's feet. I think that she's going to tell Hermione what happened. Instead, she leans over and whispers something to Rosalind that I don't catch. For a split second, Rosalind looks like she may answer back. Instead, she stands, pushing her chair under the table and grabbing her handbag. She follows the boys out of the door.

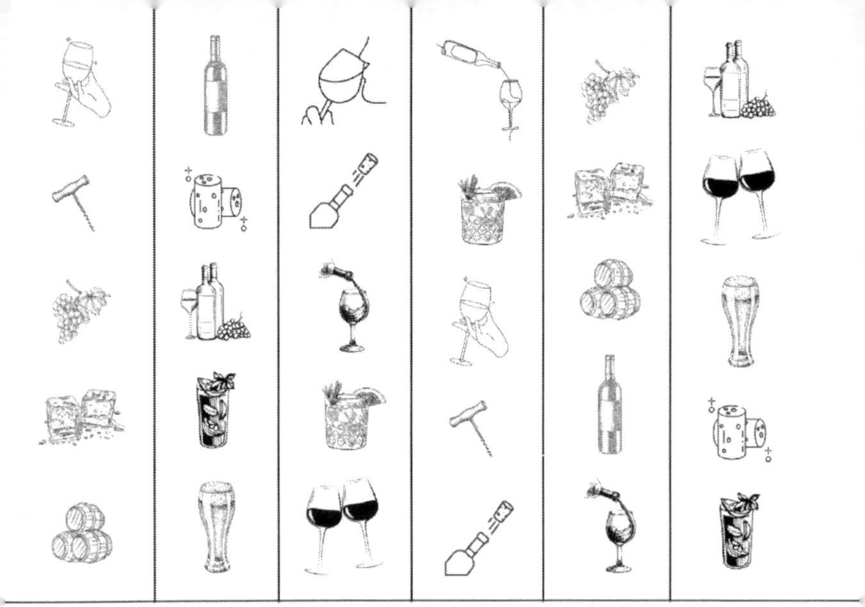

Pinot & Playhouses

Front Row Seat

Welcome back to Pinot & Playhouses where we make wine and theatre accessible to the masses. Last night, something pretty incredible happened. I got a front-row seat to a wine heist in action. Now, this one was a little different. Hear me out…

I was sitting there, at The Ivy, drinking a heavenly chardonnay when across the room from me I spot two boys who look vaguely familiar, except I'm sure I've never seen them before in my life. I'm there for the auction (blog post pending) and so I mind my own business and watch as they join a table of other patrons. These patrons, one of them in particular at least, happened to be the winning bidder on the bottle of Margaux being auctioned. They chatted for a while and as the boys left one of them grabbed the beautifully gift-wrapped expensive bottle of wine from between the feet of the new owner. One of the guests sitting at their table followed them, so I presume that everything is now in-hand. Hopefully, the bottle is now back in the hands of the rightful owner who is likely missing their prize (one they'd paid a substantial amount of money for). The boys aren't just stealing regular old bottles of wine anymore – they've progressed to ones of significant historical relevance.

I wonder where the boys will hit next, or if they'll be caught red-handed. It's funny, many of you seem to be rooting for the boys (and their tea-leafing ways) but why? They're breaking the law, right? Are you team 'the boys' or team 'the restaurants'?

Let me know what you think in the comments. Like, share, and follow Pinot & Playhouses for the latest news and tips in wine and theatre.

Cheers!

Francine (the woman behind Pinot & Playhouses)

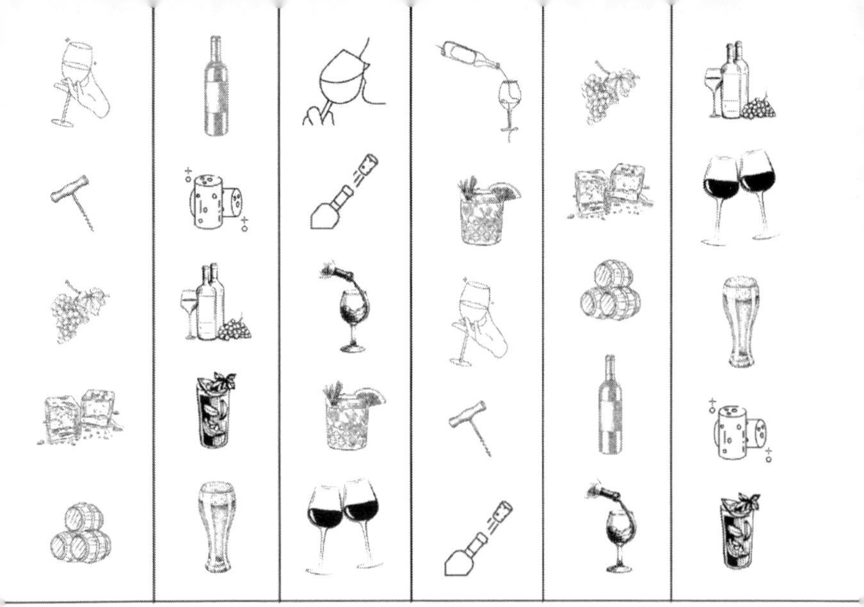

A Chance Meeting

This blog post does better than any of my previous ones. The engagement is insane. I tagged a poll to the bottom of it for people to vote whether they were team 'the boys' or team 'the restaurants' and my readers are (almost unanimously) on the boys' team. I sit and watch the comments, the votes, the shares grow until I'm convinced my eyes are deceiving me. After I uploaded the blog, I started to research Prunella Downing for a while (in preparation for our interview) until I find myself bored out of my brain. I want to make our interview different, exciting, but there are only so many tricks I have up my sleeve. Other than becoming a stage star and marrying rich (becoming a widow over ten years ago) there's nothing to sink my teeth into. At best I could maybe ask her about nepotism in show biz, her daughter Rosalind is playing a main character in Merry Wives too. Not exactly cutting-edge journalism, but something with a bit of bite. I jot some questions down and before I know it, it's dinner time. I can't bring myself to order in, and so I decide to take myself out again. What's the point in being single (and earning a decent income) if you can't take yourself out at the drop of a hat? I pretend it's not the second night in a row.

I choose a restaurant known for its wine selection, wondering if maybe I can interview a sommelier and call it work. Spirit of It is a large modern establishment, where people my age go because they think it's young and hip. In reality, the young and hip wouldn't be seen dead there. It suits me perfectly and by the time I get there at 7.15pm, it's already emptied out somewhat.

I scan the room and see plenty of available tables, but settle on one at the bar. Something about having a meal at the bar makes you feel less conspicuously alone.

The man behind the bar is a little younger than me, but not enough to make me feel conscious about my age.

'What can I get for you?' he asks.

'What wine would you suggest?' I have the wine list in hand, scanning down it. For as long as I've been writing about, and talking about wine, I still don't feel like an expert.

'Our most popular wines at the moment are a Chilean Sauvignon Blanc, a Romanian Pinot Noir, or, if you're looking for something sparkling, our Spanish Cava always goes down a treat.'

'Order the 2018 Malbec,' says a voice next to me.

I recognise him immediately. Dick, one of the wine thieves.

'And what gives you the jurisdiction?' I ask, raising an eyebrow, hoping that communicates that I know who I'm dealing with.

'Let's just say I appreciate good wine, and the 2018 Malbec is a good shout if you're not wanting to spend a fortune.'

I look back to the sommelier and he shrugs. He either doesn't give a shit, or agrees with Dick.

'Fine, the 2018 Malbec, please. Large.'

'Let's have the bottle,' Dick says.

He catches my questioning glance.

'Better value for money that way,' he says.

'And are you planning on *buying* that bottle?'

'No, but you are,' he says.

His audacity astounds me, but something about it is annoyingly charming.

Pull yourself together, I chastise myself. Not only is the, admittedly handsome, young man next to me clearly a misogynist, but he is also a wine thief. And rudely presumptuous.

'And will you be having food? If so, I'll send over a member of the waitstaff,' the sommelier says.

'Yes please,' I say.

Simultaneously, Dick says, 'No.'

'Already eaten, or too broke to pay for it?' I ask him.

'A bit of both.' The bastard winks at me. He actually winks at me.

'He'll have a menu too,' I say as the sommelier places the bottle of wine on the table, and a long-stemmed glass in front of each of us.

'Why?' he looks me up and down trying to figure out my ulterior motive.

'Maybe I'm hoping you'll spill some of your dirty little secrets if I buy you a nice meal.'

'Ah, I wasn't sure you recognised me.' He smirks like a kid who's been caught in the act.

'Busted.'

The waiter arrives with the menus. I don't need to read the menu. I always have the same here.

'The Cajun burger, please. Fries, not chips.'

'Sure thing,' the waiter says, tapping away on his tablet.

'Same for me,' Dick says.

'Awesome. Can I get you anything else?'

'No, thank you,' I reply.

'Thanks very much,' the waiter says, and leaves us alone.

'I didn't peg you as the type to eat a huge burger,' Dick says. There's a dopey grin plastered on his face.

'You don't know me,' I say. Until this moment I presumed he knew who I was. I've made a fortune writing about his wine-stealing antics. It didn't cross my mind that the person who was making me so much money might not be aware of the blog posts. Although, in all fairness, I didn't know what he looked like, or his name, until yesterday.

'I know you well enough.'

'Oh yeah?'

'Yeah, I like to keep up on current events, especially when I'm the subject of said events.'

'So why do you do it?'

'Read your blog? It's good. Funny, and highly informative.' He waits for me to bite.

'You know what I mean.' I roll my eyes, not seeing the point of hiding my annoyance.

'Oh, the wine thing?'

I don't answer. I raise my eyebrows and gesture for him to continue.

'Oh no, you don't get it that easily. Let me enjoy my meal first. I'm your cash cow. The least I can do is have a satisfying meal, and a decent glass of wine, on your dime.'

I can't find it in me to argue. He's not technically wrong.

Dick picks up the wine glass with long delicate fingers. *Pianist fingers,* my grandma would have called them. I allow myself to take in his face while he drinks. He looks normal. Completely and utterly normal. Not the kind of guy you'd worry about stealing from your establishment. He's around my age, maybe slightly younger, late twenties perhaps, but he holds himself in a way that makes him seem older at first glance. He's got the typical men's hairstyle, short back and sides, scissors on top. The front of his hair is swept back away from his face. Dark eyes, slim nose, high cheekbones. Objectively handsome, which is both irritating and likely why he gets away with stealing wine. He looks innocent. Your average guy.

The food arrives thankfully very quickly and so we don't remain sitting in silence for too long. Dick inhales the burger in three bites, but takes longer on his fries. I cut my burger into two halves and take my time. The food here is beyond delicious and so I have to savour every single bite.

When we're finished, Dick piles the plates neatly and puts them to one side. It's a gesture that takes me by surprise.

'So, about the wine?'

'What about it?' He's enjoying my discomfort.

'Why do you steal it?'

'That is a multifaceted question.'

'Care to answer it?' I push.

'Sure, answer mine first. Why did you write that Terry and me are idiots? You make us sound like we have no idea what we're doing and that this isn't a very delicate and intricate operation.'

It's a fair question. 'Well, all of my information comes from the staff at the restaurants and witnesses. All I can do is write what they tell me, and most of them made you sound like idiots.'

'Ever consider that they might be biased because we managed to steal a bottle of wine from them worth a couple of hundred quid?'

'Of course,' I reply indignantly. 'But you weren't exactly knocking my door down begging to give your side of the story.'

Dick bobs his head, considering my explanation.

'So, why do you steal wine?'

'I like wine,' he says.

'And so you steal it?'

'Yes.'

'But there has to be a reason why. Why do you think it's okay to steal wine? Why do you choose specific restaurants? What do you do with it afterwards?'

'I drink it,' he says. His eyes crinkle at the corners when he smiles.

'Dick,' I warn.

'Francine,' he says. The first time he's spoken my name aloud. 'I like wine. I can't afford to buy the kind of wine I like, so I steal it. There doesn't have to be a big cosmic reason behind why people do what they do.'

'But why risk getting caught? Why buy something you can't afford?'

He sighs, like I've somehow disappointed him. 'I won't get caught.'

'You sound so sure?'

'I am sure. I haven't been caught yet,' he says.

'But you'll get caught eventually.' I don't understand how he can be so blasé about getting caught for theft.

'Why? Why do I have to get caught eventually?'

'Because the odds are against you. You have to be caught. Eventually, somebody will be a step ahead of you, or you'll make a mistake.'

'I don't make mistakes,' he says. Anger prickles at my skin. He's infuriating in a way I've never felt before. There's no logic to his argument, and yet he fully believes what he's saying.

'So landing in the Thames was on purpose?'

'Yes.'

'Oh, fuck off,' I say. I'm unable to control the smile on my face.

Dick throws his head back and laughs. I shrink into my shirt, afraid that the whole restaurant is looking at us.

'Look, I work in a shitty job where I'm surrounded by shitty bottles of wine and liqueur. When I get the chance to try something a bit better, I'm going to jump at it.'

'Maybe you should get a better job, and then you can legitimately buy the wine?'

Dick scoffs. 'I've reached my career peak, I think. The off-licence is fine, and they don't notice when the odd bottle of wine goes missing if I'm getting desperate so…'

'Sounds like you're living a self-fulfilling prophecy. Or you're an alcoholic.'

'I like you,' he says. 'You're funny. And I would never have known. You don't come across as this funny on your blog. You kind of sound like you've got a stick up your arse.'

'Wow, thank you.' The sarcasm lies thick between us.

He shrugs again. 'Just saying it as it is.'

'Where's the other one? Terry?' I ask, pretending I don't know his name.

'He's on a recon mission at the moment. That expensive wine we stole last night, the bottle went missing, and I want it back.'

'Very expensive seems to be an underestimation of just how expensive that wine was.'

'Yup. It was Terry's idea. Normally we tend to opt for the slightly cheaper ones, petty theft rather than anything more serious. But Terry's not necessarily, well, he ain't the brightest bloke. Nice guy, but, well… Anyway, we managed to leave with the bottle, as you know. And Terry brought a lovely lady home with us. Rosalind, I'm sure you saw her too, seeing as you were spying on us…'

'I wasn't spying on you,' I say, although I know it's pointless to argue, because I was.

'Okay, darling, sure. So, Terry brought this bird home with us. She was all over him in the taxi. It was, well, hot and heavy. When we got back to the apartment—'

'—you live together?'

'Yes, we do. Living in London, on minimum wage severely limits our options. Can I continue?'

'Where does Terry work?'

'C U Next Tuesdays. He's a shift manager. Can I continue now?'

'Sure.' I mime zipping my lips.

'We got home, ate some cheese, and drank the wine. It was out of this fucking world gorgeous. Was it worth that amount of money? Maybe not. But it went down a treat. I then retired to my room and left Terry to it with Rosalind. When I got up the next morning, the bottle was there, on the windowsill. Completely empty, but the way the sun caught it, it shone symbols all over the room. Like the light refracted into it and cast little pictures on the wall. I snapped a photo to show Terry in case the sun went in before he got up, sometimes that happens. I went in the shower, but when I got out the bottle was gone, as was Rosalind. But why? Why would you steal the bottle?'

'Maybe because her aunt ordered it, so technically it is hers?'

He considers this for a moment. 'But it's an empty bottle.'

'Maybe she saw the patterns you mentioned, and she thought it was pretty, so she took it. Can't blame her really. Or maybe she believes the legends?' If anybody was entitled to take the bottle, no matter how *pretty* it was, it was Rosalind.

The fact that Dick seems to think he's been bested in some way makes me question his sanity.

'Here,' Dick says, thrusting his phone under my nose.

'Woah,' I exhale. The photo on his screen shows what looks like the walls of his living room. The light from the window shines through the deep green wine bottle and refracts, just like he said, symbols onto the wall. I zoom in on the photo and stare at the hieroglyphs plastered across his wall.

'That's insane. You've answered your own question though. That's why she wanted it.'

'But why didn't she ask to take it?' Dick says, leaning close like he's managed to get one over on me.

'Because you were in the shower and Terry was asleep, and she wanted to sneak out of there without talking to you.'

'Fair,' he says.

'Maybe you could try to figure out what the hieroglyphics mean and go on a treasure hunt?' I'm only being half-sarcastic.

He turns away from me. 'Oy, Terry!'

Terry shuffles through the door and over to us, empty-handed.

'Hello Francine,' he says.

'Hello Terry,' I reply, which earns me a smile from Dick.

'What a weird coincidence. Did you just happen to be here or are you following us again?' Terry says.

'I've never followed you. Last night was a coincidence, just as this is.'

'Sure, whatever you say,' Terry says. 'I think she's got a soft spot for us. It's not often stalkers are as gorgeous as Francine here, so I'll take it.'

I don't respond, and attempt not to be flattered by the compliment.

'Did you get it?' Dick asks, ignoring Terry's comments.

Terry looks at me for a moment before shaking his head. 'She wouldn't give it back to me.'

'How come?' Dick asks.

'She said it belonged to her auntie, that she paid for the wine and therefore the bottle is hers.'

I attempt to contort my face into a mask of humbleness, but fail miserably.

'Don't,' Dick warns me.

'I wouldn't dream of it.' I smirk, sipping my wine and enjoy being right.

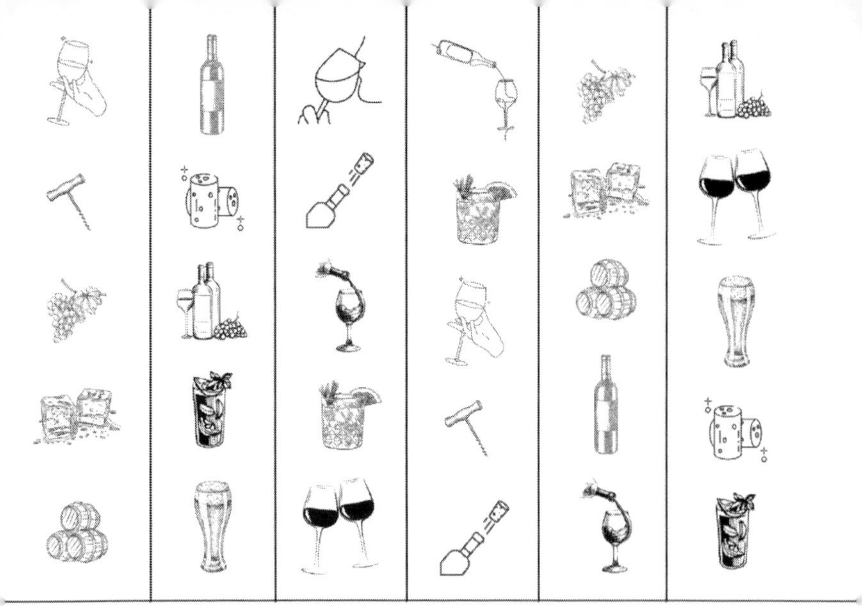

Practically Perfect in Every Way

I sit in Prunella's living room, bone china in hand, and smile. I've never been in a house quite like Prunella's before. It screams 'old money'. The sofa that I'm currently perched on looks like it might be older than me. I want to say it's baroque style, but I was never one for that kind of thing. I don't know my arse from my elbow when it comes to antique furniture. All I know, is that it fits the rest of the house perfectly, from what I've seen so far, the entrance hall and the *parlour.* I'm surrounded by things I daren't touch.

'Are you happy for me to record the interview?'

Prunella sits opposite me, on a chair that matches my sofa perfectly.

'Yes, of course,' she says. The smile on her face is almost as false as mine. Mine is to hide how uncomfortable I am. I believe hers is because, like most *serious actors,* she hates interviews.

I set up my phone to record and place it on the low coffee table between us, that looks like a cup of coffee has never been anywhere near it.

'Ready?' I ask.

'Go ahead,' she says.

'This is a beautiful home,' I say. 'How did you choose the décor?'

'Thank you. Most of the décor is family heirlooms that were passed down to me by my grandfather, the late Earl of Cadogan, George Walker. After his death, I had my pick of the furniture, and I chose most of it. A few bits and pieces belonged to my mother too. She had impeccable taste. Unfortunately, she died when I was a little girl. Having all her treasured possessions around makes me feel close to her.'

'I'm sorry to hear that,' I reply. I already knew that, of course. I did my research, but what else do you say when somebody mentions their dead mother?

I reel off my list of questions, asking about her career (demanding work but worth it), her proudest achievement (her daughter, Rosalind), and her plans for the future (to continue on the stage for as long as she is able). Her answers are succinct but well thought out. She's been schooled in interview techniques, likely by one of her agents, and it works for her. She comes across as kind, professional, and comfortable in her skin.

'And how did you find yourself in show business?' I ask.

'I've always loved books and film. As a little girl, my nose was forever stuck in the pages of a book. I read anything and everything I could get my hands on. I was ravenous for it. And then, when I was a little older, my father, Professor Donald Radcliffe, took my sister and I to see a production of Othello on the stage and I was absolutely enraptured by it. The atmosphere, the talent, and creativity. I came away from it wanting to make other people feel the same way I felt that day. After that moment, I begged my father to take me to every stage show he could. We practically lived at the theatre, and he was happy to indulge my fancies.'

'You mentioned your sister. Can you tell me a little about your relationship with her?'

'Yes, my sister is the very successful Hermione Radcliffe, she's the head of classical studies at the University of London, and she's currently part of the effort that's bringing the Nefertiti exhibit to the British Museum.'

'You must be proud of her,' I say.

'Very,' Prunella says. I note that she doesn't elaborate any further, and that her only comments about her sister relate solely to her job. I have a split second to decide whether to push the subject or not, sensing Prunella's reluctance. I decide against it. This is my first serious(ish) interview, so I don't want to push my luck.

'You mentioned that your father was a professor? What field did he study?'

'My mother and father were both in the field of Egyptology. They actually met in Cairo in the late 1940s. My father worked for New York University. My mother studied at Oxbridge prior to meeting him. My father was very keen that we knew both of our heritages and so we lived between New York and London.'

'So, you come from a strong line of academics?'

'Yes, I do.'

'Tell me something nobody knows about you,' I say, hoping that this may be my in, something that sets this interview apart from her many others.

'Hmm, let me think for a moment.' She pauses and takes a gulp of her tea. 'Oh, okay, I've got it. I've had the same breakfast every day since I was a little girl. Jam on toast. You can't go wrong with jam on toast.'

A stream of swear words fills my mind, but still, I manage to smile.

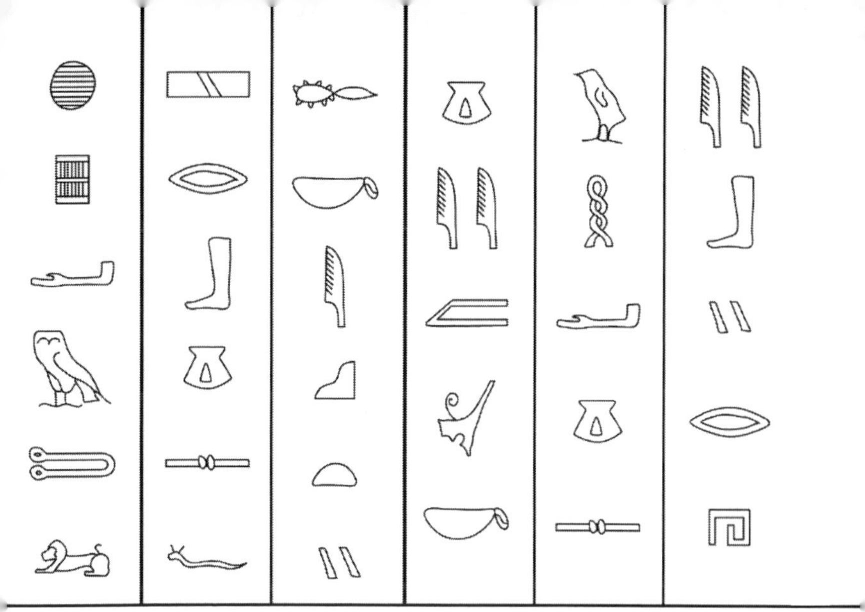

The Daily Vine: The Internet's Premier News Agency

Death of ANOTHER Egyptologist

There has been another death at the QUEEN NEFERTITI: THE ROYAL TOUR exhibit. Farouk Al Mohammad, from the Egyptian Heritage Foundation, was poisoned while delivering a lecture on responsible archaeology. This is the same manner of death inflicted upon Professor Abu Hinksley, who passed away two days ago. The deaths are being investigated by

Detective Wicks, who is well established in solving high-profile 'suspicious deaths'. The exhibit has once again been closed to the public while the investigation into the crime scene is underway. However, it is thought that it will open again tomorrow.

There are many difficulties surrounding investigating a death in such a well-trafficked area – so many visitors pass through the doors to the British Museum on a daily basis, making the number of potential suspects and also the validity of evidence difficult to navigate. When asked for comment, Detective Wicks stated, 'We do not believe these deaths put the general public at risk. However, if you are visiting the British Museum, please remain vigilant and contact security if you witness anything suspicious. Further, we would encourage you not to drink anything you didn't see poured/made. I wish to reiterate, there's no need to panic and once the exhibit reopens, you will be able to visit as usual. You will see a larger security and police presence, purely as a precaution.'

For further information on the exhibition…

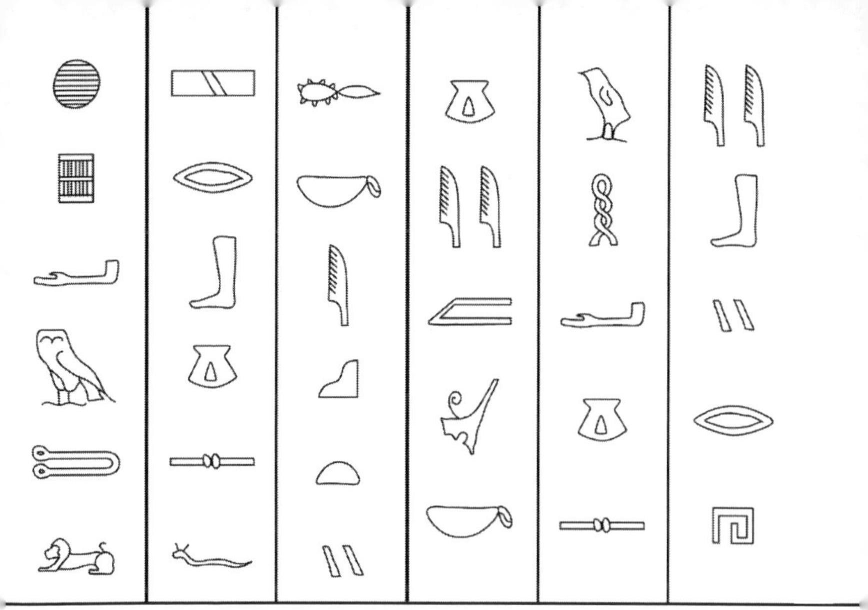

Risky Business

Another Egyptologist has died. The strange thing is that it doesn't seem so much like news, as gossip filling the mouths and ears of Londoners. Murders aren't necessarily uncommon in the city, but the fact that two people from the same group have died under the same suspicious circumstances, and in a very public way, has set the people's tongues wagging. The general consensus around town is that if you're not an Egyptologist, you're safe, and so people are more than happy to continue visiting the exhibit, which has just reopened this afternoon.

The press has been all over Hermione Radcliffe, Gillian Cox, and Martin Van Bussell, the remaining three public figures involved in the Nefertiti exhibition. Each has given their own statements, with varying degrees of openness and clarity.

'We have been assured that the exhibit is safe to continue,' Hermione said to one reporter.

'It is unfortunate that the deaths of our colleagues are detracting from the nature of the exhibition,' Gillian Cox said to a different reporter. 'Nefertiti is a feminist icon and one that we can all stand to learn a lot from. I am saddened by the passing of two deeply knowledgeable and respected gentlemen in the field, but let's not forget that we're here to celebrate the life and leadership of Queen Nefertiti, who ruled Egypt as an equal…'

'No comment,' Van Bussell is quoted to have said.

With each passing hour, the detective in charge of the case seems to age. With each quote, each press conference, and each voyeuristic photograph taken, his shoulders hunch further and extra crow's feet are added to his eyes. With two very public poisonings, I am not envious of his job.

Like the rest of the public, much to the annoyance of Gillian Cox, I presume, I'm enthralled. Who would target seemingly mundane academics? I've set up a Google alert on my phone so that I'm always up to date with the very latest information.

There's almost a magic to the whole thing. The Ancient Egyptians were steeped in mystery and legend. There's still so much about them that academics don't know. We can't even be entirely certain of the colour of their skin, for instance. Which, it transpires, is something that one of the dead Egyptologists, Professor Abu Hinksley, was somewhat of an expert on. Much of his research surrounded whether known Ancient Egyptian historical figures, such as Queen Nefertiti, were Nubian, or of a lighter skin tone. This was the subject of fierce historical debate. Some reporters even went as far as to suggest that this unchangeable opinion was the cause of Hinksley's death. That was until Farouk Al Mohammad, whose only contentions lie in the fact that he believed all the Ancient Egyptian artefacts belonged to the Egyptian people (and their government), and that their excavation amounted to theft. There's an, admittedly small, part of me that wishes I'd studied the classics back in college or university. It's all very interesting.

The press is desperate for any new clues and developments linked to the deaths. Unfortunately for them, they don't have a link to one of the Egyptologist's sisters. *This* may be just the angle that my Prunella Downing interview needs to take in order to thrust it out of the box of stereotypically boring actor interviews. As such, I schedule myself another visit with Prunella, determined to get the scoop on Hermione Radcliffe. It may be a little underhand, but what I have so far is dull enough to bore me to tears.

Once again, I find myself standing on the immaculate path that leads to Prunella's considerable heavy wooden front door. As I reach up to press the doorbell, the door flies open, and Rosalind almost walks straight into me.

'Hi,' I stutter. 'Sorry, I was about to…' I gesture to the doorbell.

'You're here to see my mum?' she asks. Her auburn hair is swept back in a sleek bun. The fair skin around her eyes is mottled red. It doesn't take a genius to realise she's been crying.

'Yes,' I say, wondering if I should ask whether she's okay.

'This way.' Rosalind turns on her heel and walks back into the house.

'Were you leaving? Did I catch you at a bad time?' I ask.

'No, it's okay. She's in here.' I'm led down a hallway and into the dining room. A mahogany table eats up the space. There's barely any way to walk around it. Prunella sits at one end, looking minuscule against the sheer size of the table. In front of her is an open copy of a book. She has a pencil in hand.

'Good afternoon,' Prunella says, standing to greet me.

I shuffle awkwardly around the table and shake her hand.

'Thank you for seeing me again at such short notice.'

'No problem at all,' she says. Either she's an incredible actor or she really means it.

'I just have a few more questions, and I'll be out of your way.'

She holds out her arm and indicates to the chair next to her. I pull it out and squeeze into the gap. I'm not a large person by any means. I work hard in the gym and eat well. I maybe overindulge a little on wine, but I'm on the toned side of average. The table is far too big for the room.

'Is this another heirloom?' I say.

'The table and chairs?' she asks.

I nod, and she responds, 'Yes, they belonged to my grandfather.'

That makes sense. I suppose. Personally, I would have forgone the heirloom in favour of something that fits, but I understand her wanting to make their bequest a centre piece.

'It's beautiful,' I say. I'm telling the truth. It looks like something out of *Downton Abbey*. I can't even begin to imagine how much it would cost.

'Thank you. I love it. It's one of my favourite pieces.'

'You have a lot of heirlooms. Do you have a favourite one?'

'That's a tough question. I suppose it would have to be my mother's necklace.' Prunella tugs at her collar to reveal a delicate silver chain with a tiny heart locket attached to it. 'It reminds me of her. I never leave home without it.'

'How sweet. That's a gorgeous necklace. Your mother must have had good taste.'

'Oh, she definitely did.' Prunella smiles fondly.

'It's very different to the other heirlooms,' I say. I'm not entirely sure what I'm getting at, but it strikes me that every other heirloom she's pointed out is a dated piece of furniture.

'Probably why it's my favourite,' she smiles.

'Ready for a couple of questions?'

'Go ahead,' she says. Something that is impossible to miss about Prunella is her posture. I don't think I've ever seen a person sit (or stand) so straight. It makes me painfully aware of my own posture. I push my shoulders back and press 'record' on my phone.

'Your sister has been in the news recently. Two of her colleagues have died in suspected poisonings at her exhibit. What's your take on this?'

She's not expecting the question, but she remains composed.

'What has happened at the museum is a terrible tragedy and I worry about my sister's, and her remaining colleagues', safety.'

'Have you been in contact with Ms Radcliffe?'

'I saw her the other night at the wine auction. She seemed to be handling the whole affair as she always does. She's a strong and stoic woman. Hermione will not let this phase her.'

'Who do you think is behind it?' I ask.

'Behind what?' I can visibly see her prickling.

'The deaths,' I say.

'How should I know? My sister and I live very separate lives.'

'How come?' I ask. I'm pushing too much. I know it. I need to step back a little or Prunella will close down completely.

'We have vastly different interests. My sister travels a lot for work, and I work around the clock for my theatre shows. We're ships in the night, so to speak.'

'That's a shame…' I say, leaving the sentence hanging.

'It is what it is. I'd rather not comment anymore on that. If you have any questions about the deaths, you'll have to ask Hermione. I assume that's why you came back.'

'I'm sorry. I didn't mean to overstep. I just wanted you to be able to air your opinions.'

'That's okay. Do you have any other questions for me? About the Merry Wives or my career?'

'Yes,' I say, sheepishly, and reel off a list of boring questions with the aim to put her at ease.

When we're finally done, I stand and shimmy towards the door. Prunella stands to follow me.

'Please. I can let myself out. I really appreciate you allowing me to follow up with you today.'

'It's been a pleasure,' Prunella says, re-opening her book, *A Dead Man in Deptford,* without any further prompts required.

'Have a lovely day,' I say and make my way down the never-ending hallway and to the front door.

I catch a glimpse of it immediately. The light from the windows surrounding the door hits it perfectly, refracting a green light around the hall. It sits on a sideboard that wouldn't be out of place on the Titanic. The magnum bottle is impossible to miss. It stares at me, daring me to take it. There's something about the bottle that has needled under my skin. The legend, the theft, the deaths of the Egyptologists. I feel like I'm an extra in the latest Indiana Jones film. I grab it and walk out of the door, my heart beating at a hundred miles an hour in my chest. The adrenaline that's coursing through my system tells me it's the riskiest thing I've ever done.

I pride myself on being rational and level-headed and yet I've just stolen something from an interviewee. I half-run back to my car and by the time I hit the driver's seat, I decide it's too late to second-guess my decision.

Who the hell am I?

What the hell have I just done?

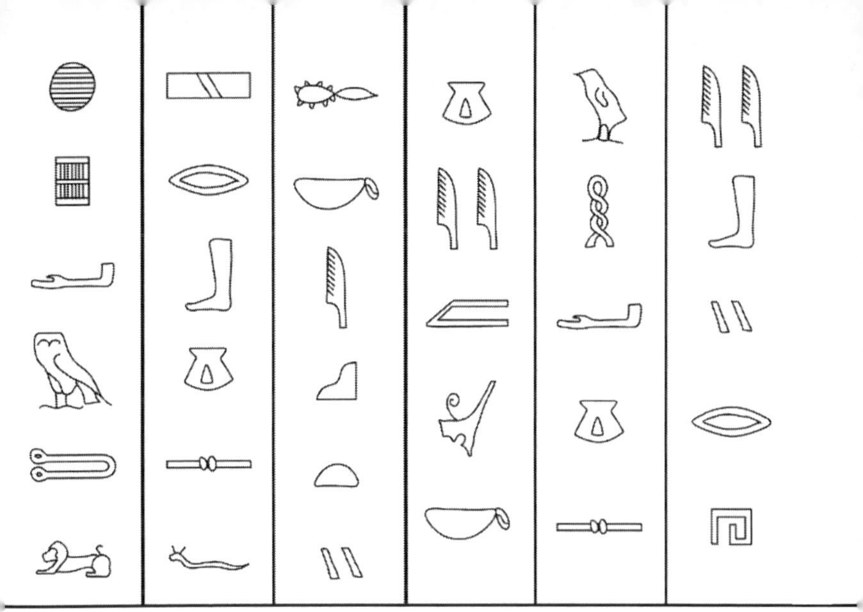

Spidey Senses

I park in Bloomsbury Square. The bottle is nestled into my passenger seat. I strapped it in so that it wouldn't fly off the seat if I had to brake abruptly. I shake my head at my stupidity. This isn't me. I don't do things like this. My gut tells me that there's more to this story. The bottle, the theft, the boys, Hermione and Pru, the murders of the Egyptologists. I don't know. I'm not usually one for gut instincts. I trust my head, not my gut. And for some reason, my gut has seen fit to lead me astray. Next thing I know, I'll be pulling off a wine heist or something stupid. I read an article once that said if you committed one crime, it's like the seal has been broken, and it's so much easier to commit the second one. It alters your brain chemistry. As I climb out of the car, I make the decision to put the bottle in the boot until I can figure out what to do with it, and then I head off to the British Museum.

Hermione Radcliffe is my target. If I could ask her a couple of questions, then I know I could put a great article together. It's an extra bit of spice to add to my interview with Prunella. As much as I wanted to move more into serious journalism, interviewing Prunella (a very serious actor, of course) about her life wasn't quite what I had in mind. I had hoped, somewhat naively, that Prunella would let something slip that would take the article to the next level. She hadn't. And so, I now had to rely on Hermione to do that. Prunella may not be happy about sharing the limelight with her sister, but I've made my peace with that. Sometimes, on the way to the top, you had to step on a few toes. And my spidey senses were tingling, telling me that I *had* to talk to Hermione.

As I walk through the doors of the British Museum, a blast of cool air from the air conditioners hits me. At each side of the door, framing it like two Grecian statues, are security guards. Milling around the lobby are a few uniformed policemen. They look uncomfortable, like they're not sure how to behave in a museum. A sign points right to the Nefertiti exhibit. I follow it, my heels clicking on the marble floor. The museum is a beautiful old building. The perfect place to show off Nefertiti's wares in all their glory. Grand, opulent, and regal. The exhibit takes up most of the left wing on the ground floor. Surrounding it, are many of the museum's own pieces that remain year-round. In essence, it's a full floor dedicated to Egypt, and it is magnificent.

The first thing that hits me is gold. Within many of the glass display cases are gold artefacts, decorated with deep royal blue and black. And there, at the very centre of the room, is the bust of Nefertiti. I find myself unable to tear my eyes away from it. She really is a stunning piece of art. Beside her is a card explaining the piece and its relevance.

The bust of Nefertiti is a painted stucco-coated limestone bust. We believe it to have been created in 1335 BCE by the sculptor Thutmose. To this day, it is one of the most prolific, and copied, pieces of art from Ancient Egypt. The piece was discovered in 1912 in the sculptor's workshop by a team led by Ludwig Borchardt. Despite laws at the time restricting the removal of artefacts from Egypt, the archaeological team disguised the bust with clay and smuggled it out of the country. There is still much contention about the ownership of this artefact. We at the British Museum are honoured to house it here for the duration of the exhibition.

Until now, I'd never really considered the ownership of artefacts. It had never crossed my mind that *somebody* owned the museum pieces. I'm internally aware that I'm personifying an inanimate object, but I find myself feeling saddened that the bust was ripped away from its own country and people all because some rich, white man wanted it. A story that is as old as time. And one which could be applied to all facets of life, I suppose.

I work my way around the rest of the exhibit admiring the artefacts. The Standing Figure of Nefertiti stands proudly at the centre of the second atrium. It stands at only 40cm tall and doesn't quite cut as imposing of a figure as the bust, but it is still an impressive sight. Having been found broken, and expertly put back together, some parts of the statue are still missing or damaged. A home altar, depicting Aten (the sun god) at the centre, with Akhenaten and Nefertiti, with their children provides a rare insight into the king and queen's private lives. Many other reliefs are displayed throughout the exhibit. They paint a story of a respected and worshiped couple, who ruled equally and started a monotheistic religious revolution, progressing from worshipping many gods, to one. Aten, god of the sun, I learn, is usually depicted as a sun-like disk in representations.

It's all very interesting and I feel like I'm reading from the pages of a fairy tale rather than walking around a, slightly too-cold, exhibit. The last artefact to catch my attention is the Amarna amulet. I vaguely remember it being mentioned during the interview on *Wake-Up & Shake-Up*. I've never been one for jewellery, but the amulet is breathtaking. It's easy to imagine it around Nefertiti's neck. Funnily enough, it looks just like the necklace Hermione wears. It makes sense that she would style herself after Nefertiti. It's cute, like a little kid wanting to dress like their mother, or a pop star. Instead, Hermione wants to dress like Queen Nefertiti, which is arguably the perfect attire for an Egyptologist. The information card tells me that there are many Amarna amulets, but this one is *THE Amarna amulet.* It is the be-all and end-all. The top-dog. And it is suspected that it hung around Queen Nefertiti's neck, which is incredibly cool, if you ask me.

Found by Penelope Radcliffe in 1952, the Amarna amulet is a prime historical artefact. The amulet is depicted in many of the reliefs and figures of Queen Nefertiti. It is therefore suspected that she wore the amulet throughout much of her life. It is the most recent artefact in this exhibit and one of the last objects relating to Nefertiti to be found. Legend says that the amulet holds the power to control the minds of others. However, this has not been proven. The Amarna amulet is a symbol of beauty and strength, still in near-pristine condition. It signifies the stalling of the search for Nefertiti. Since this date, we are no closer to finding her burial chamber, sarcophagus, or mummy. A few months after the Amarna amulet was discovered, the Egyptian government took control of the nation's archaeological sites and museums. Since this day, progress has stalled.

'Beautiful, isn't it?'

I turn and find Hermione standing behind me. Her perfume is the first thing to hit me, a strong woody smell. Amber? Patchouli? She's wearing a linen suit and looks the very picture of a professional older woman. Up close, I can see the lines that delicately decorate the skin around her eyes.

'It is,' I say. 'I can see where you got your inspiration.' I nod to the amulet hanging around her neck.

'It goes with every outfit I own,' Hermione says, breaking into a smile. 'I'm Hermione Radcliffe, one of the organisers of this exhibit. My mother discovered that necklace. It was her greatest achievement in life.'

Did I detect a hint of jealousy? 'Yes, I,' I begin, unsure of whether to admit that I know full well who she is. 'I'm a fan of yours. I watched your interview on *Wake Up & Shake Up*. I have a segment—'

'Yes, I know who you are. Ms Francine Witt, the face behind Pinot & Playhouses.' She reads my confused expression and says, 'I like budget wine as much as the next person.'

'Wow, thank you.'

'I saw you watching our piece on *Wake Up*, you left before I had the chance to tell you I was a fan of your blog.'

I chastised myself for being shocked that Hermione read my blog, she didn't seem the type to spend a lot of time scrolling on her phone, much less reading a bougie blog about wine. I had to stop making snap judgements about people.

'Funnily enough, my family and I actually fell victim to those pesky wine thieves. You wrote about it on your blog. I didn't know you were at the auction.'

'I was covering it for work.' I say. I hold my breath, wondering whether she's about to tell me off for not notifying the authorities after witnessing the event. I toy with the idea of asking why Rosalind would steal back the wine bottle from the boys and why it would have ended up on Prunella's sideboard, and consequently in my car. Something about the wine bottle is still bugging me though. Maybe the fact that it is currently in the boot of my car after I stole it from a leading stage actor.

'It was very disappointing, I have to admit. You heard the legend behind the bottle. Many of us old Egyptologists believe it might be true. The theory is that it leads to some priceless artefact smuggled out of the country just after the coup. It is a shame.'

'I can imagine,' I say. I'm sure that my face is burning bright red, showing my guilt.

'Anyway, there's nothing I can do about it now. It's been reported to the authorities, but you know what they're like with theft. It isn't a priority, especially with the deaths of my colleagues. Murders should certainly be the priority, but it doesn't stop me from feeling disappointed. It would have made a nice addition to the exhibit too.'

'I'm sure it would. You've done an amazing job with the exhibit, by the way. It's incredible.'

'We've worked really hard to pull it together.' She falters, like there's something else she almost says.

'I'm sorry about your colleagues,' I say, taking my moment.

'Thank you. It's unfortunate but I'm thankful that we can keep the exhibit open. The last thing dear Abu and Farouk would have wanted would be for the exhibit to close. They were both extremely proud of it. It is a shame that we have to have such high security and police presence, but needs must.'

'Are the police any closer to finding out who did it? Or why?' I lower my voice as I speak, like I'm spreading gossip on a playground.

'The police won't tell me anything,' she says.

'That's a shame. Do you have any idea who would do it?'

'None at all. My colleagues were well respected. Yes, their ideas may have been considered partisan by some, but nothing that would warrant their death. Who in their right mind would want to kill an Egyptologist?'

'That was my thought exactly,' I say.

'Ms Radcliffe?'

Hermione turns to look at the man who has soundlessly appeared behind us. Detective Inspector Wicks, I recognise him from the news.

'*Doctor* Radcliffe.' Hermione corrects him and crosses her arms over her chest.

'I have a couple more questions for you. Let's talk somewhere a little quieter,' he says.

'It was lovely to meet you, Francine.'

'You too,' I reply, watching Hermione being led away by the detective.

Down the Rabbit Hole

The wine bottle feels like a presence in my flat. No matter where I place it, I can feel it looking at me. It's disconcerting, to say the least. I've picked my phone up multiple times to call Dick to tell him that I've rescued the wine bottle. On some level, I'm concerned that I did it because I'm attracted to him, which would be absolutely ridiculous. Dick is a thief and a conman, one who has no right to the bottle of wine that he stole (which is the pot calling the kettle black, I suppose) but he was also funny and sweet and, admittedly, kind of hot. I'm now at that age where I always thought I'd be married, at the very least. My biological clock is ticking so loudly that it should be illegal. I may as well have a sign across my forehead saying 'EGGS EXPIRING SOON. COME AND FERTILISE ME!' And yet, I know that in modern society, it doesn't matter. There are plenty of ways to have a family without having to settle for a man. Especially a man like Dick.

I distract myself by researching Nefertiti. Since I visited the exhibition earlier, I cannot get her out of my mind. There's a magic to the mystery surrounding her missing burial chamber, sarcophagus, and body. It's the one significant remaining mystery of the Ancient Egyptians. Such a prominent figure in the country's history, and her body has still not been discovered, despite numerous (and very expensive) archaeological efforts.

In my research, I stumble across an article co-written by Penelope and Donald Radcliffe, Hermione and Prunella's parents, about the mystery of Nefertiti.

Nefertiti: More Than a Pretty Face

By Penelope Radcliffe and Donald Radcliffe (1955)

Nefertiti is an unknown enigma, to this day, despite our best efforts. The dates of her birth and death are unknown. Relative to other ancient monarchs, we know very little about Queen Nefertiti. Initially, upon the discovery of her bust in 1912, much focus was placed upon her beauty. She was hailed the most beautiful figure in ancient history by many. When you factor in that the archaeological monopoly at the time was that of the rich, white man, the skewed perspective is clear. A beautiful queen had been discovered, surely she was only a pretty face and had no impact other than to stand by the side of her pharaoh, Amenhotep IV, who later became known as Akhenaten.

The legacy of Nefertiti and Amenhotep IV would remain buried for millennia. A revolutionary ruling pair, who transformed Egypt from polytheism to monotheism, research suggests that their reign was treated with much disdain in the immediate aftermath with their capital (built by the pharaoh) being abandoned and much of the artwork depicting the duo being defaced. After their death, Egypt returned to polytheism.

Prior to the breakthrough of Nefertiti's bust being discovered, she was assumed to have played a supportive role in Amenhotep's reign. We have since established that this is a vast understatement of her role within the monarchy. After Amenhotep changed his name to Akhenaten and began his campaign to convert Egypt to the worship of the sun god, Aten, Nefertiti was promoted to an equal position to that of her husband. In essence, she was to be worshiped just as he was. And, therefore, she was seen as superior to every queen that had come before her and gifted her own temple. Nefertiti was in no supporting role, she was in an equal partnership.

Together they ruled all of Egypt and were worshiped by the people, treated as gods upon earth. However, their reign was filled with contention. Threats from foreign lands were evident and despite being in the wealthiest era of its history, Egypt's wealth began to falter. The creation of a new religion and a new capital drained the wealth the pharaoh had inherited. Their reign lasted for 17 years, until Pharaoh Amenhotep (Akhenaten) died at the age of 40. His death marked a turning point in Egyptian history and what happened next is the subject of much debate – much of which would likely be solved with the discovery of Nefertiti's burial chamber. The aftermath of the pharaoh's death saw many monuments and statues dismantled and destroyed, all of which would have been crucial to further our knowledge of their history. The destruction of artefacts is one of the greatest issues facing historians.

The discovery of Akhenaten's burial tomb was significant in piecing together our understanding of Nefertiti as she appeared throughout the murals lining the walls. There is some debate about whether, just prior to his death, Akhenaten promoted his wife to co-king allowing her to rule in his wake as Ankhkheperure Neferneferuaten, guiding Egypt into the reign of Tutankhamun (her stepson). While this theory does have credit, should it be true, Nefertiti gained no recognition for her political leadership during this time, even though it would have been partially her rule that restored Egypt to its former wealth.

But herein lies the mystery…

Where is Nefertiti?

Alongside many other archaeologists well versed in Egyptology, we have searched tirelessly for Nefertiti, yet her final resting place is yet to be found. There have been many false positives over the years, with highly professional and respected historians believing beyond a doubt that they had discovered her tomb. The Valley of the Kings has been combed, as has much of Amarna, and the Boundary of Stelae of Akhenaten, and she's nowhere to be found. It is a mystery that we aim to solve in our lifetime. Having discovered the Amarna amulet, we feel that we are ever closer to bringing Nefertiti to the people. Nefertiti is often overlooked as an icon of strength and leadership. It wouldn't be remiss to call her the original feminist. She took Egypt, and the patriarchy, by storm.

It is our hope that Egypt opens up their hearts to us once more so that we can continue searching for the beloved queen. Archaeology should always be a community endeavour and preventing foreign experts from lending their professional opinions and guidance will only lead the search for Nefertiti to stall, and that would be a disservice not only to Egypt, but the whole world. History belongs to all of us. We hope that the Egyptian government will see sense and allow us to support their archaeological efforts moving forward. We may still find Nefertiti in our lifetimes.

I resist the urge to shave my head and let my armpit hair grow as long as it pleases. Nefertiti has reignited my feminism from beyond her (missing) grave. It's easy to see where Hermione gets her devout Nefertitiism (yes, I just created that word) from. I'm half considering joining her cause and retraining as a historian. Although, that does sound like a lot of work and I'm already careening towards midlife with a terrifying quickness.

I'm just about to go and change into my pyjamas and spend the night watching documentaries about Ancient Egypt (damn you Hermione) when my phone rings. Dick.

'Hello,' I answer.

'Are you busy tonight?' he says, straight to the point. I appreciate that.

'Well…' I begin. It looks a little sad if I admit I have no plans.

'I'll take that as a no,' he says. I can hear his smile through the phone. 'Can I take you out to dinner? I owe you.'

I spend a moment too long considering my answer. Did I want to go on a date with Dick? Long term, he's not the ideal mate. But short term, it could be fun.

'Hello?' he says, sparking me into action.

'Yes, sure why not. As long as you promise not to steal any wine. I will not be a part of your con.'

'I wouldn't dream of it.' This time he laughs aloud.

'Fine then. Where would you like to meet?'

I arrive at The Broken Puppet, a restaurant that I've never been to before. It sells exclusively Italian food, which I love. But the wine list looks like shit, if we're being honest here. Dick promises me it's a hidden gem, but I'm not entirely convinced. The décor is dated, the tables are sticky, and I'm questioning whether this date is worth it. Dick arrives ten minutes late. Behind him trails Terry. So, not a date then. I try to ignore the disappointment that sits in the pit of my stomach. I remind myself that I'm a strong woman who doesn't need a man. Especially a liability like Dick.

'You're late,' I say.

'Yeah, well, I'm a criminal so what did you expect?' Dick winks.

'He's never on time,' Terry interjects, sitting next to me. Dick sits down opposite.

'So, what's this about?' I ask.

'We missed you,' Terry says.

That earns a smile from me. Bloody hell, both of them are charming. It's so easy to see how they get away with their criminal propensity. They charm their way through life without a care in the world.

'That, I believe,' I say.

'Well, Terry here is having some relationship trouble and we wanted a woman's perspective on the matter,' Dick says.

'Rosalind?' I ask.

'Yeah. She won't return my calls or texts. It's like our night of passion never happened.'

'Maybe you're shit in bed,' I suggest.

'No, that's not it,' Terry says, adamantly. 'I've had a lot of practise.'

'He has,' Dick concurs.

'Your personality?' I say.

'Nope, not that either,' Terry says.

'He's a charming bloke,' Dick adds.

'Maybe because you're a thief? She's kind of out of your league.' My final suggestion. Rosalind was upper middle class, at the very least. And Terry, well, Terry wasn't.

'It's wine, not the toys of sick children.' Terry makes a face like I've said the stupidest thing he could possibly imagine.

'And we only steal really good wine,' Dick says.

'Then I'm out of ideas,' I say.

'I told you she wouldn't know,' Terry *whispers* to Dick.

'Then why did you come?' I shoot back. I'm enjoying the argument. It's banter, friendly, at least I think it is.

'Dunno, bored, and desperate.' Terry turns his attention to the menu, and I turn my attention to Dick.

'He really liked her,' Dick says. Terry kicks him under the table and the cutlery bounces. 'What, you do!'

'Some things just aren't meant to be. You can't make somebody like you.'

'Why not? Everybody else likes me.'

'Everybody?' I push him. He takes the bait.

'Yes. Everybody.' Terry crosses his arms like he's done arguing.

'That's true,' Dick says. 'Terry never has a problem with the ladies.'

'Is that why this is bothering you so much? Because Rosalind is the first to reject you?'

'No,' he says too quickly.

'Right,' I say.

'So, you have no advice?' Dick says.

'Other than to find somebody else because she's not interested?'

'Other than that,' Terry says.

'Nope, I'm fresh out of advice.'

'I need a cigarette,' Terry says.

'But we haven't ordered food yet,' Dick says.

'I'll have what you're having,' Terry directs to Dick. He pats his pockets. 'I need a light. In fact, I need a cig. You got one?'

'Don't smoke,' I say at the same time Dick says, 'No.'

'Fuck,' Terry says. 'I'll try those classy birds.'

He walks over to a group of posh older women. They're plastered in foundation two shades too dark and wearing heels two inches too high. They seem the type to drive their kids to football matches in Chelsea tractors.

We order food from a waiter, and Dick asks for a bottle of the Zinfandel that costs less than the meal. Terry vanishes out the door with the group of women.

'Trust me,' he says when I raise my eyebrows.

The wine arrives first, and Dick pours me a glass.

'Wow, okay,' I say, picking up the bottle and looking at the label. 'This is nice.' I'm unable to keep the shock out of my voice.

'I know,' he says, a smug look sweeping across his face.

I bring the glass back to my mouth to take a sip as Terry comes bounding back to the table.

'Reckon you can make yourself scarce tonight?' he says.

'Why?' Dick takes a lazy drink of his wine. We both know why Terry wants their home to himself, but he's making Terry work for it.

'Look, they *all* want me, Dick. All of them. I'm about to sleep with at least four women at once. At least! Do you know what kind of an opportunity this is? I can't pass this up, and you'll be in the way.'

'What are you planning on doing to my house?' Dick says. 'Can't I stay in my bedroom?'

'No, Dick. No, you can't. I'll be in the living room. There's no way I can fit all these women in my bedroom. Don't ruin this for me.'

'Where do you want me to go?' Dick says.

'You'll find somewhere. Thanks for being a mate.' Terry slaps Dick on the back and turns to walk away.

'What about your meal?' Dick says.

'Share it with Fran,' Terry says and he's out of the door before I can blink.

'So, where are you going to go?' I ask, teasing Dick.

'I dunno. Usually, there's only one bird so Terry stays in his room. But… how many did he say? Four? How on earth is he going to manage that? I'm tired just thinking about it.'

'I suppose you'd better find a nice bench to settle on.' I smile and take a sip of my wine.

'Yeah, I better had. Or find a bar that's open all night. The last thing I want to do is catch Terry in the act by going home too early.'

'Well, you can always sleep on my sofa, if you'd like.' I say the words before I think of their ramifications. It sounds like I'm propositioning him.

'Thanks. I'll take you up on that.' There was no pause, like he was expecting me to offer. 'It's the least you can do seeing as I pay for your flat,' he says.

'I can change my mind,' I say.

'Yeah, but you won't.'

He's right. I won't.

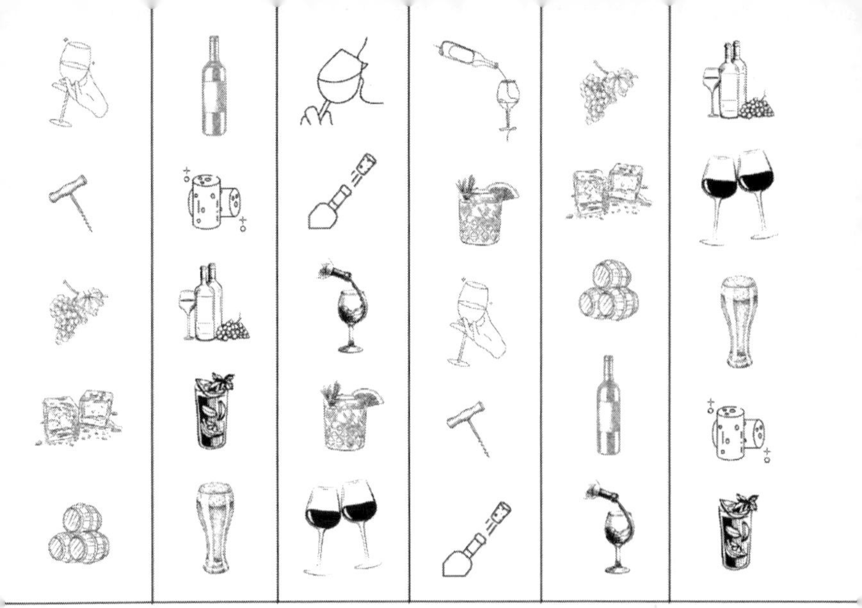

A Night to Forget

I wake up next to Dick. Memories of last night come flooding back to me. Shame shades my skin a deep red. What did I do? I never sleep with guys on the first date. And last night wasn't even a date. Not that I have any issues with women who do sleep with people on the first day – you do you, girl power – but it's not me. Dick snores gently, facing away from me. His dark hair is tousled, his shoulders are bare. I pray to any god that's listening that he's wearing his boxers. I don't even have the excuse of drinking a lot. I had two glasses of wine, that's it. That's less than I do most nights.

I'm not sure who made the first move. It seemed like we both did. A simultaneous decision. The second we stepped through the front door, his lips were on mine.

I attempt to slip out of bed before he wakes up, but the movement of the quilt causes him to stir. I would have liked to have downed a decent amount of caffeine before we attempted to make small talk, but it looks like that was a pipe dream.

'Good morning,' Dick says. He pushes himself into a sitting position, leaning back against my headboard like he owns the place. He rakes a hand through his hair, messing it up. *Why the hell does that make him look hot?*

'Morning,' I say.

We sit in silence, both feeling suitably awkward.

'About last night,' I say.

'Don't worry. We don't have to speak of it again.' I don't know whether to be insulted or relieved.

'I was going to ask if I could put a play-by-play on my blog,' I joke. 'I'm sure my readers would love to know what the notorious wine thief is like in bed.'

'I'd end up batting the women off with a stick. Go for it,' he says.

'Wow, somebody is big-headed,' I laugh. 'Coffee?'

'God yes,' Dick says. He climbs out of bed. He's naked. Completely naked, and he doesn't even have the decency to try and hide it.

I thank my lucky stars that I had the forethought to pull on the oversized t-shirt that I usually sleep in last night.

I walk to my kitchen trying to pretend that there isn't a naked man in my bedroom. I switch on the coffee machine and wait for the coffee to drip into the jug.

Dick saunters into the kitchen and sits at my small bistro set. Thankfully, he's dressed, once more in last night's clothes.

'Nice place you've got here.' He scans the open-plan room. It's my kitchen, dining room, and living room, each sectioned off in a way that makes it flow. I *love* my flat.

'Thanks,' I say, silently begging the coffee machine to speed up.

'Wait, is that?' Dick is up and out of his chair before I turn around. 'That's my bottle,' he says.

'Shit, yes, I…'

'Why have you got it?' There's no anger in his words, just confusion.

'I did an interview with Prunella Downing, Rosalind's mother, and it was just there. I don't know what came over me, but I just grabbed it. I meant to tell you, but I forgot…'

'My sexual prowess caused you to forget about it?' Dick picks up the bottle and holds it aloft, inspecting it.

'Sure,' I concede.

'Why did you take it?' he asks.

'Honestly? I don't know. It was a split-second decision. There's clearly something to it if everybody keeps stealing it, myself included. I took it before I thought it through.'

He nods, pursing his lips like he's an antique dealer evaluating its value.

'Wait. Hold it there,' I instruct.

Dick does what I ask and holds the bottle in place. The light from my window hits the bottle and casts hieroglyphs onto my walls.

'Woah,' I breathe. It's magnificent.

We both stand and stare at the characters currently plastered all over my wall.

'What if they really do mean something,' I say. 'Maybe we should try to decipher them? If the legend is true, we could find some buried treasure.'

'If you want,' Dick says. He doesn't sound convinced.

'Let me take some more photos.'

Dick holds his pose as I take too many photos.

'So, what do we do with her now?' Dick says. He lowers the bottle and cradles it to his chest like a baby.

'*Her?*'

'The bottle. Do we share custody? That would be the responsible thing, right? To co-parent?'

'Tell you what, I'll keep *her* for now and I'll do the heavy lifting and translate the hieroglyphics, and then you can take your turn. How's that sound?'

I have no intention of giving the bottle back to Dick, but he doesn't need to know that.

'Perfect. I've always been better in a supervisory role anyway,' Dick says. 'Now, about that coffee?'

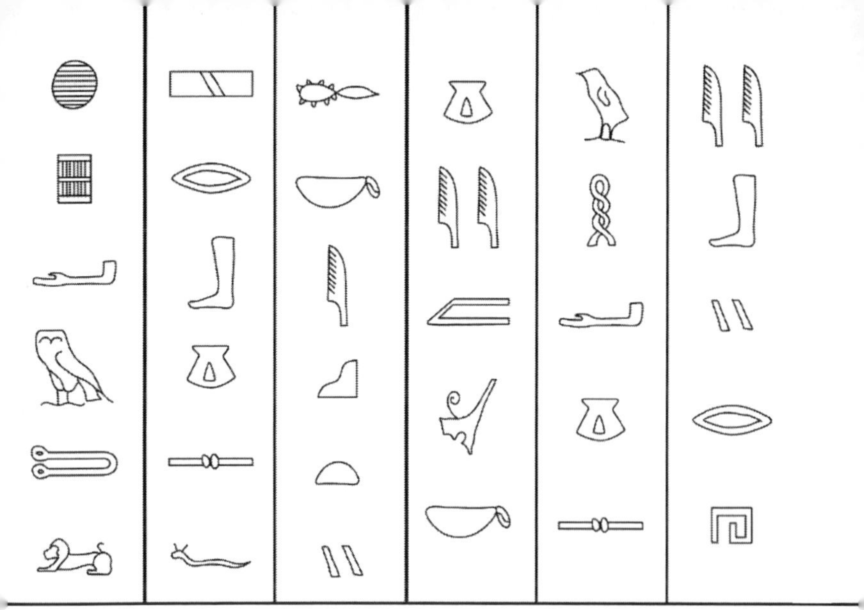

Master of Puzzles

When Dick finally leaves, after the longest shower I've ever known a person to take, I get down to the business of cracking the code on the bottle. My photographs are clear, and, from them, I manage to draw the hieroglyphs down on a piece of paper. I soon find myself drowning in the complex world of Egyptian hieroglyphics. I had, wrongly, thought that each hieroglyph corresponded with a letter of the alphabet. Oh, how I was mistaken. Yes, hieroglyphs are a form of pictorial writing, but they're far more complicated, and therefore annoying as hell, than that. Egyptian hieroglyphs are split into three categories: logograms (that represent a word), phonograms (that represent a sound) and determinatives (symbols placed after a word to clarify the meaning). Therefore, my simple little project turned out to be a pain in the arse. Which, incidentally, could have been written about a million different ways in hieroglyphics, not to be hyperbolic or anything.

The symbols on the bottle repeated over and over.

I trace the hieroglyphs. Each one has multiple meanings.

The first symbol is an *ankh*, sometimes referred to as the Egyptian key of life. The second, I have a bit more trouble with. It is the symbol for the spirit, or sometimes the soul, or sometimes a bull. This doesn't narrow things down particularly well. The third is the symbol for a brazier with a flame. Usually meaning *fire*. The final two symbols appear to be a house or building, and a cup. The cup is the only one I'm fairly confident about.

So, we have a key of life, spirit/soul/bull, fire/cooking, a house/building, and a cup. Not particularly useful. The annoying thing about hieroglyphs is that they're highly dependent on the person who crafted them and their own interpretations of what they meant. The bottle doesn't seem to have any determinatives, as far as I can tell, and so that means that the hieroglyphs are either logograms or phonograms which, again, leaves me with far too many possibilities. I moan aloud and put my head in my hands, wishing I'd taken up cryptic crosswords as a hobby. My current plan of action is to throw ideas at the wall and see what sticks. I start with the phonological idea, with each hieroglyph representing a letter.

I try different letters that the symbols could suggest: LSFHC, LBCBC, KSBCF, and so on. None of them look even remotely like words, nor do they sound like words when I say them aloud in my empty flat. There's the possibility that the hieroglyphs could just be random, meant to decorate the bottle, but that doesn't make sense to me. There are far prettier hieroglyphs to choose if you were using them just for decoration. It seems to me like they mean something. I'm not entirely convinced that the legend is true, that the hieroglyphics are a treasure map, but I'm not totally against the idea either. I decide to delve deeper into the meanings of each of the symbols, with the hope that something will come to light.

The ankh is a recognisable symbol to this day, even if people are unsure what it means. It was often used to refer to life, living, nourishment in Ancient Egyptian texts. However, more current translations link the ankh (the key of life) to treasure or sustenance. It has been found etched onto the burial chambers of many Egyptian kings and queens to signify the treasure, gold (and occasionally servants and pets) that they are buried alongside, with the hope that these things will accompany them into the afterlife. Taking this symbol at face value, it likely means some form of treasure or provisions. However, given the fact that I am by no means an expert on Ancient Egyptian, it could mean something entirely different (or nothing at all).

The next symbol along is usually called the *Ka*. The Ka refers to the soul of a person, what remains after their death. There have long since been mistranslations that the symbol refers to something being doubled, because of the two arms, but this has been proven to be incorrect. The reason for the occasional translation to *bull* appears to be due to the anthropomorphic representation of Ka which is a man with bull horns atop his head. The Ancient Egyptians definitely didn't make things easy for themselves. I decide to forget the bull translation, for now, considering it unlikely. So far, I have life/treasure, and soul. Then the symbol for fire or cooking. And the final two – house/building and cup.

The treasure is in the soul, in a building, in a cup, on fire?

The life and soul, building and a warm cup?

A fiery life, soul, home, and drink?

I throw my head back and close my eyes. I'm beginning to hate the Ancient Egyptians. Of course, that isn't entirely true. I blame them for being so interesting that I'm sitting here on an evening attempting to translate hieroglyphs on a wine bottle. That's what I need, a glass of wine.

I head to the kitchen, pour myself a large glass of Pinot Noir, and sit back down on my sofa. The notepad in front of me is full of my scribbles, crossing outs, and other almost unintelligible thoughts. The wine bottle is from 1943 and was only drank from a couple of days ago. The wine held within the deep green bottle had remained that way for over fifty years, meaning that whoever carved the hieroglyphics into it, likely did it in the 40s or 50s. This particular bottle of wine vanished off the radar until a couple of months ago, when the auction was organised.

The wine had been a favourite of the archaeologists in Egypt in the late 40s and early 50s. My research told me that crates of the stuff had been transported to Egypt, and other archaeological sites, for decades. This particular Margaux was the wine of choice. Other than that, the wine itself had nothing to do with Egypt. It was bottled in Margaux. One of the archaeologists, or at the very least somebody that lived there at the time, had to have carved the symbols into the bottle. A secret message in an ancient language that only a few people would understand. That *had* to mean something. Why else would somebody painstakingly carve the markings onto the bottle?

I spend the next hour staring down the hieroglyphs and challenging them to reveal their hidden meaning. They do not do me the courtesy of showing their intended meaning. There's one person who I know for sure would be able to translate them fairly accurately. Hermione. I wish I'd have got her phone number or email address when we chatted earlier, but that ship sailed. It gives me another excuse to go back to the exhibit to try and catch her. I'm still in shock that she knows who I am, and that she reads my blog. It's a very small, and very crazy world we live in.

I open up my laptop once again and see if there have been any recent updates on the murders of Hermione's colleagues. The fact that two men, prominent within their industry, were murdered in broad daylight, in front of witnesses and nobody has yet been charged with the murder strikes me as odd. Usually, when there's an excess of public attention on a case, the police are very quick to demonstrate that they have suspects in custody. But not this time. That doesn't mean they don't have their suspicions, of course. They may just be playing it safe and building a rock-solid case against a person. But who?

Throughout all the news articles and blog posts, there's no mention of a suspect.

Who would want to kill an Egyptologist, and in such a public way?

If it were a single murder, you could argue that it was a personal vendetta against the victim. However, because there's been two murders, it stands to reason that the second murder was to throw the police off the trail or that it's a person with a vendetta against Egyptology. And surely there's nobody on the planet with a vendetta against Egyptology. That's just ridiculous. It's like having a vendetta against the Ancient Greeks.

Unless… My brain clicks into journalist mode, and I begin to consider all the motives for the murders that I can think of. A few ring too close to home.

1. It brings publicity to the exhibit.
2. It removes academic competition.

3. In a male-dominated field, two men have been taken out of the running.
4. The world is talking about Nefertiti once more.
5. The only people who would benefit from the deaths of Egyptologists, are other Egyptologists.

As though on cue, a news article pops up. *BREAKING NEWS. Hermione Radcliffe escorted into custody for questioning. Detective Wicks has yet to comment.*

The article doesn't tell me much more. Only that an hour or so ago, Hermione was escorted into Wick's police car (a black BMW) and taken to the closest police station for questioning. She has not yet been released, as far as I can tell. The journalist wants shooting, as far as I'm concerned. There is no evidence as far as I can tell that Hermione is being anything other than helpful. And the journalist is painting her as a murder suspect. That's irresponsible, to say the least. Although, Hermione is in the unique position that she would gain from the deaths.

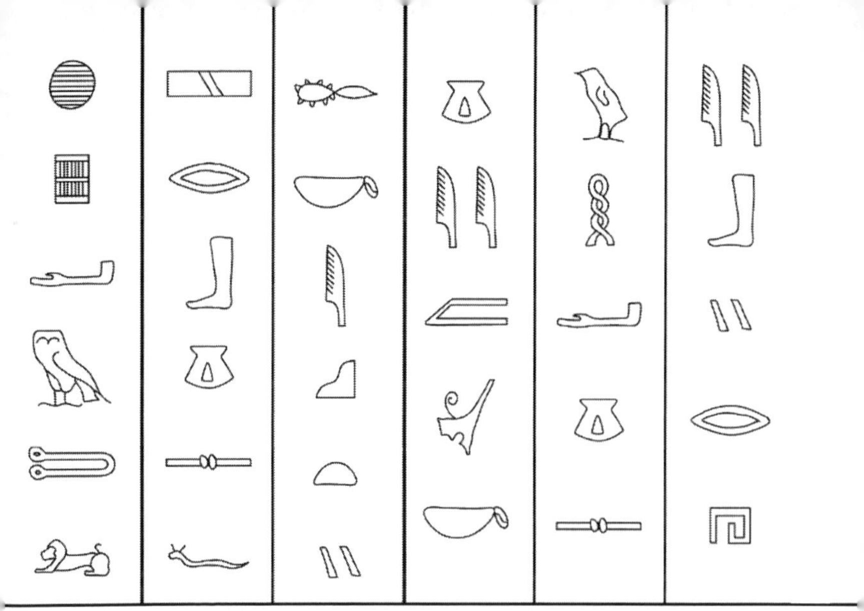

An Unlikely Encounter

I set off bright and early the next morning, in search of Hermione. While her release wasn't quite as big news as her being taken in for questioning, I did find a later addition to one of the articles that said she was released just before midnight. I know better than to believe that's a good sign. It's neutral, at best. My plan is to hang around the exhibition until she shows up. After a late night, I would expect her to show up late. I would. I have a photograph of the hieroglyphs on my phone to show her. Hopefully, she won't mind my line of questioning. Last night, I dreamed of (not Manderley again) but of wine bottles and hieroglyphs. I can't get it out of my damned brain. If Hermione can help me translate it, then I have this strange feeling that I'll be able to put it all behind me and I'll be able to move on with my life. I still haven't written Prunella Downing's interview up yet. The prospect of writing it, without so much as a tiny smidge of excitement or interest, is driving me insane. There's a small part of me that's hoping maybe Hermione will let something slip today that I can tag onto the article, to make it stand out just a little. Anything at all would do. At this point, I'm just desperate not to write another boring-as-hell actor profile. But if the subject of the article just happens to be boring, then there's not much I can do to spice it up and keep my journalistic integrity.

I park up and walk over to the museum. The building is almost as staggering as the exhibitions held within its walls. It makes sense for a museum to be this beautiful. It seems only right.

'Excuse me.' I turn and find Rosalind standing before me. In her hand, she holds a manila envelope.

'Hello, Rosalind,' I say. 'Are you here for the exhibit? I was actually hoping to have a word with your aunt.'

'No, I'm here for you.'

'How did y—'

'You need to read these. My mother isn't who she says she is. Use this in your write up, but please don't mention where you got them.'

She pushes the envelope into my hand. My reflexes close my fingers around the package.

'What is it?' I ask.

'Just read them, please. I'm sorry. I have to—'

Looking flustered, Rosalind turns and walks away, bumping into other pedestrians like a pinball.

I'm about to open the envelope when I decide it would be best to tackle one thing at a time. I push the envelope into my leather work satchel, one of my favourite things I own, and head in search of Hermione.

I notice her immediately, the amulet around her neck catching the sun and refracting little rainbows of light around the room. She waves at me, and I take that as my cue to walk over to her.

'I was hoping to bump into you,' I say.

'You're not after a quote, are you? Reporters have been badgering me all day.' She seems tired, although she tries to laugh it off.

'No, of course not. But I do have a favour to ask.'

'Go ahead,' she says.

'Could you translate these for me?' I hold up the hieroglyphics on my phone.

'Where did you get these?' she asks, pushing a thin pair of wire glasses onto her face.

'From the Margaux bottle,' I say. I choose not to lie to her.

'Oh.' Her eyes widen. 'Do I want to know how you got your hands on that bottle? Is this for a blog post about the wine thieves?'

'No, and kind of,' I reply.

'Okay,' she smiles kindly. 'I will, of course, translate them for you but you need to send those photographs to me. I am the rightful owner of the bottle after all, but I only require the hieroglyphics for now. When you're done with the bottle, I would appreciate it if you could return it to me. You're bloody lucky I'm a fan of your blog.' A smile teases at her lips.

Feeling suitably chastised, I pull out my phone and send the photos to Hermione.

'Thank you,' she says. 'And you'll give the bottle back to me when you're finished doing whatever it is you're doing?'

'I promise,' I say.

'Fine, well, let me take another look.' She pauses to study the hieroglyphics again 'These hieroglyphics are a bastardisation of Ancient Egyptian. I would argue that it was done by somebody with only a basic understanding of the language. You see, because of the nature of Ancient Egyptian, translating the hieroglyphs can be immensely tricky. Each scribe has their own bias, and that makes it an incredibly difficult language to translate. However, this is written in such a way that we would write in English. Straight across from left to right, with one character following the next. Then there's the symbol for fire. This usually means what it says on the tin. Fire, burning, cooking, that kind of thing. The final two letters are initials, for a name or a place, I believe. H and C. The first two, I would argue mean *treasure* and *soul.* Treasure can be written in a few different ways and the fact that this person chose to use the ankh to symbolise it would suggest that they believe this treasure would ensure a person would be set for life, so to speak. Now, Ka, as in soul, that's a tricky one. In this context, I'm not sure what it could mean.'

Hermione pauses for a second, studying the phone. 'These two symbols aren't ones that we'd usually see in such close proximity as they are two different sides of life. The ankh represents the living body, and the soul represents what remains of us after our body expires.' She purses her lips. 'I think the only way to know what these symbols mean together would be to ask the person that wrote them.'

'That's what I was afraid of,' I say. 'I appreciate your help.'

'You're more than welcome,' Hermione says. 'I do apologise, but I have to rush off. My colleague is leading a seminar group in a little while and I'd like to sit in.'

'Of course. Thanks again.'

Hermione walks out of the room, leaving me torn. To take another wander around the exhibit, or to go and write up Prunella's interview. A very easy decision, it turns out.

I take a lap around the exhibit, pausing to look at some items of clothing that historians believe Nefertiti once wore.

A commotion behind me stirs me from the clothes. There's a thud and a crowd of people move in waves to the corner of the room, next to a display of ancient crockery. My feet move without my instruction, taking me to the growing throng of people.

On the floor, is Professor Van Bussell. Somebody is leaning over him doing chest compressions. His face is already weirdly expressionless.

'Call an ambulance,' somebody yells.

I watch as at least ten people put their phones to their ears.

Within what feels like seconds, the paramedics arrive. They exchange a glance that is easier to interpret than the hieroglyphics. Van Bussell is dead.

A policeman in an ill-fitting uniform walks through the door and addresses the crowd. 'Ladies and gentlemen, can I have your attention, please? The exhibit is closed. On your way out, can you please leave your name and number with my colleague at the door in case we have any further questions for you? Thank you for your cooperation, can you all please—'

'What's happening?' Hermione walks into the room and straight into Detective Wicks who has appeared out of nowhere, as though by magic.

'Ms Radcliffe, I'd like you to come with me.'

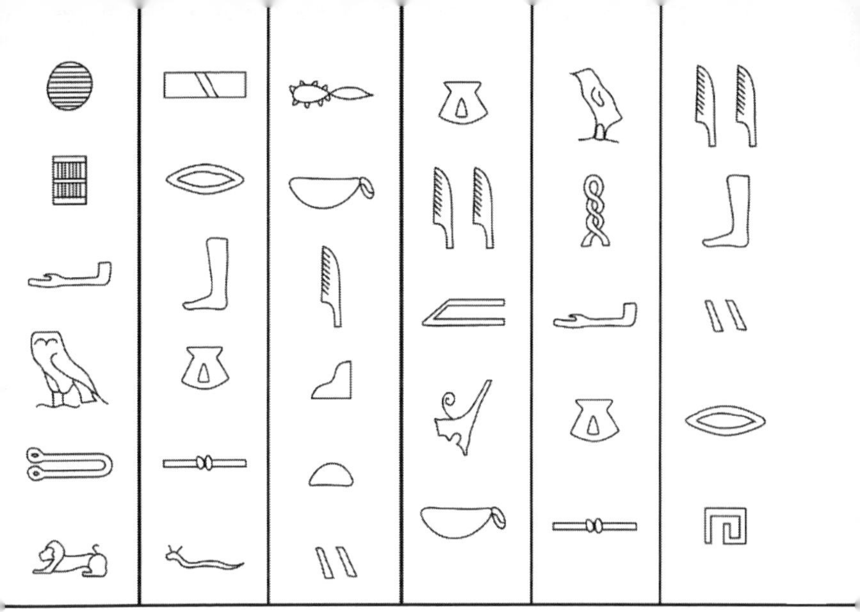

The Daily Vine: The Internet's Premier News Agency

Death of A THIRD Egyptologist

And then there were two. Only an hour ago, reports started coming out of the British Museum regarding the death of Professor Van Bussell, an Egyptologist working on the Queen Nefertiti exhibit. While we don't have any information into the cause of death yet, as it's still a very recent incident, we could be forgiven for suspecting that the death may be related to the murders of two other Egyptologists who worked on the exhibition. Farouk Al Mohammad and Professor Abu Hinksley have both been killed this week in front of crowds at the exhibit. At this stage, we have no further information on whether the exhibit will close. Although, it has to be acknowledged that there seems to be a significant safety risk for the academics working on the exhibition. We will update as more information comes to light.

BREAKING UPDATE:

Doctor Hermione Radcliffe has been arrested in connection with the murders of two of her colleagues, Farouk Al Mohammad and Abu Hinksley. We still do not know the manner of death of Professor Van Bussell.

BREAKING UPDATE:

Gillian Cox, author of the book The Female Pharaoh, and colleague of Hermione Radcliffe has refused to make a comment to the press regarding Dr Radcliffe's arrest.

BREAKING UPDATE:

Professor Van Bussell's death is being treated as suspicious says Detective Wicks. He has acknowledged that Dr Radcliffe is also a person of interest. But has not commented on whether she is being held in custody, or whether she has been charged.

BREAKING UPDATE:

The exhibit will remain open.

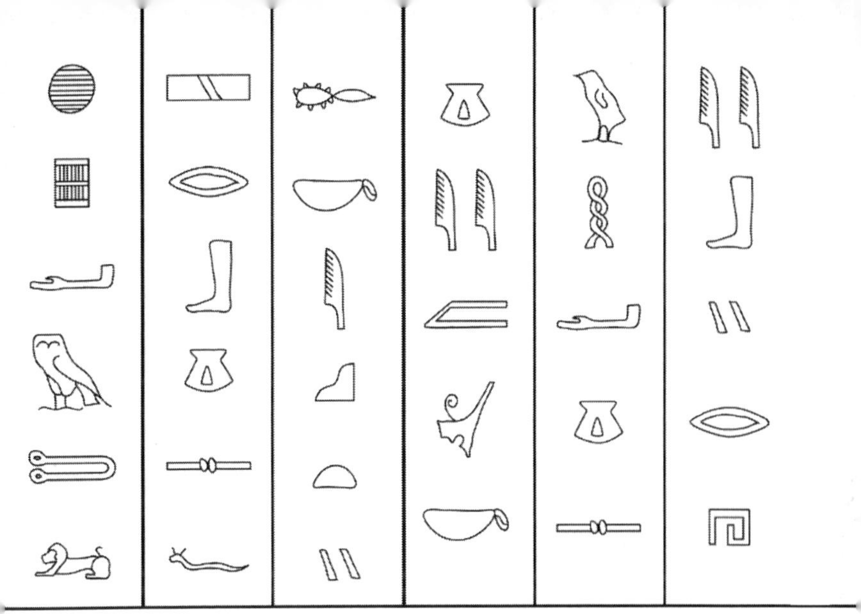

Visitation Rights

I'm still reeling that evening. I've never witnessed a person die before. It's disconcerting, leaving me feeling unnerved and off-kilter. I find that I am unable to think of anything else except Van Bussell collapsed in a pile on the floor. The latest tabloid gossip suggests that he was murdered in the same way as his two colleagues. Poison, but how could that be possible with all the new precautions in place? And why on earth is the exhibit still open? None of the general public has been harmed, yet, but surely, it's only a matter of time before somebody gets caught in the crossfire. It's better to be safe than sorry, in my opinion.

My mind alternates between Hermione being led away by Detective Inspector Wicks, and Van Bussell. I'm not entirely sure which scene I find the most upsetting: Hermione, a woman of high stature and regard in her community, being treated as a suspect, or Van Bussell's limp body. As much as the journalist part of me knows that she is a highly credible suspect, I just can't see it. Nothing in her nature suggested to me that she was capable of murder. But, then again, my instinct isn't always to be trusted.

I cannot concentrate on work, Prunella's interview has dropped to the bottom of my priority list for the moment, but I really must find time to look through the information Rosalind handed to me. Writing an interview about a theatre actor seems so superficial in the middle of everything else that's occurring at the moment. More than ever before, I'm suffering from a lack of purpose. I can feel an existential crisis on the horizon. As a 30ish-year-old woman, these crises of faith happen regularly. *What am I doing with my life? Is this all there is? Does my career even matter? What's the point of it all?* I once read in a magazine that these internal conflicts are due to astrology – when we reach the age of twenty-seven, Saturn Return throws everything out of whack. I'm not one to subscribe to astrology, but since the age of twenty-seven, my life seems to want to prove this astrological phenomenon to be correct.

I scroll through endless news articles outlining the demise of the Egyptologists, wondering if I should be worried for Hermione and the other woman, Gillian Cox's, safety. Alarm bells ring in my mind repeating – *three down, two to go.*

I decide to check out Gillian's social media. Thus far, it's been radio silence, but she's usually very active, most authors are nowadays, it's a necessary evil of the career. And there it is, the update that I've been waiting for. Gillian has posted a photograph of herself and Hermione at what appears to be a conference of some sort. They're standing shoulder to shoulder, smiling at the camera. Hermione has a good few years on Gillian, who looks like she's stepped out of an episode of *The Real Housewives of…* Hermione wears a flowing linen suit, and Gillian wears a fitted skirt and blouse. They look like polar opposites, except for their obsession with Queen Nefertiti, of course.

Beneath, Gillian has written a caption…

Over the past few years, I have had the pleasure to call this fierce woman my colleague and friend. While I am unable to comment in detail about the ongoing investigation into the deaths of our beloved, and respected, colleagues Martin Van Bussell, Abu Hinksley and Farouk Al Mohammad, I am confident that the police will find the culprit responsible, and that culprit is NOT Dr Hermione Radcliffe. She has my full support and I back her 100%. I wish that the circumstances were different and that I didn't have to post this online. But, in order to help quash the rumours that Hermione has anything to do with these deaths, I wished to share my perspective with you all.

Thank you for your ongoing support at this time. I urge any of you, if you know anything at all that may help the police, please get in touch with them. The sooner we catch the real murderer, the sooner we can go back to celebrating Queen Nefertiti in all her glory, which is what my colleagues would have wanted. Thank you. XOXO, Gillian.

It's nice to see Gillian supporting Hermione. Us women have to stick together.

My phone's ringtone pulls me out of the rabbit hole I was falling into.

Dick.

'Hello,' I say.

'I would like to visit with my bottle,' he says. 'As we have joint custody, I think it's only fair that I am able to visit with her.'

I shake my head, not bothering to hide my smile since he can't see me anyway. 'Sure, why not. When would you like to see her?'

'Now? I'm outside your building.'

I look myself up and down from my position on the sofa. I'm in a pair of jogging bottoms and my hair is scraped back from my face. Usually, before seeing people, I like to make myself look semi-decent, but if Dick is already outside, I don't have time to do that. There's a small part of me that wants to tell him to wait until I've tarted myself up, but the feminist part of me overrides it. Fuck it. I don't owe anybody *pretty*.

'Fine, I'll buzz you in.'

I peel myself off the sofa and go to press the buzzer. A few moments later, Dick is at my door.

'I brought wine,' he says, walking in like he owns the place.

'Did you pay for it?' I ask.

'Maybe it's better if you don't ask questions like that,' he says, laughing at his own joke.

'Fine, whatever. Glasses are in the cupboard.' I point in the direction of the glasses and Dick takes two out, pouring two glasses of deep burgundy wine.

'What are we drinking?'

'Shiraz, a 2015 vintage.'

'Cool.' I decide not to ask for further information. If I'm drinking stolen wine, which I'm pretty certain I am, it's better not to know the gory details. I take a sip and savour the flavour.

'Nice, right?' Dick says.

'Yes, it is. The bottle's over there, by the way. Just, try not to break it, okay?'

'That's fair.' He walks over to the bottle, still placed next to the TV. 'Did you manage to crack the code?'

'Oh, I did, yes.' My conversation with Hermione about the hieroglyphics had all but vanished from my head in the craziness of the day.

'And...'

'I went to ask Hermione Radcliffe, and she said that the hieroglyphics were written by somebody who only has a basic understanding of Ancient Egyptian. She thought it might have been written by an English speaker.' I tell him her translation of the symbols.

'Hmmm,' Dick says. 'Interesting.'

'It's either a real treasure map or somebody went to great lengths to convince people that it was. To me, it seems like one of those scavenger hunts.' I say aloud, before I can stop myself. 'You know the kind you'd do as a kid, one clue leads to the next. I don't know, something about it feels like that. Otherwise, the symbols are just random, and why would you put random symbols on a bottle.'

'True,' Dick says. 'I presume you know that Hermione has been arrested, right?'

'Yes,' I say, waiting for Dick to elaborate on his question.

'It just seems weird to me. This whole thing with the bottle – the hieroglyphs on it – and the fact that Egyptologists are dying left, right and centre. The timing seems too much to not be a coincidence. Or, maybe Hermione is a murderer, and you should stay away from her, just in case.'

'Oh, are you worried about me?' I tease.

'The police have to have due cause to arrest her, right? So maybe it's worth keeping your distance until this blows over.'

'Does that mean yes?' I push, punching him gently on the arm.

'Behave yourself,' he says.

I laugh and take another sip of wine.

'On a serious note,' I say. 'I was there when she got arrested. I saw Van Bussell die. It was… It was tough.'

'Fuck, Fran, I didn't know. Shit.' He reaches out to me and wraps me in a hug. The warm musty scent of his clothes makes me feel safe, protected. *He's a thief,* I remind myself, pulling away.

'I'm okay. I just, I can't see Hermione as a murderer, can you?'

'I don't really know her. Other than that meal she was at. She seemed nice, kind of uptight, but nice. But murderers are always the people you least expect, right?'

'But why would she kill her colleagues?' I ask. I reserve my thoughts for after I've heard Dick's perspective. I want to see if our opinions line up.

'They're her rivals, right? And they're men. She's one of those radical feminists, isn't she? Or she looks like she is and talks like she is. Maybe she doesn't like men researching a feminist icon. I don't know, there are loads of reasons to kill a person, aren't there?'

'This is three people, not one.'

'Good point. Three *male* Egyptologists all working on the same exhibit. That seems like too much of a coincidence. It has to be somebody who is involved in the exhibition – just think about the publicity. I saw something online that said the Nefertiti exhibit has been the most profitable exhibit the British Museum has had in years. All publicity is good publicity, which is, incidentally, how I reconcile with stealing wine from restaurants. You post about them, great publicity, and I get a decent bottle of wine.'

There's a quiver to his lip as he speaks. I need a cold shower. I shouldn't find this guy attractive. I shouldn't. He's the exact opposite of what I need in my life. But, damn, that smile.

'You think somebody would kill three people to bring publicity to an exhibit?'

'Not an exhibit, a feminist icon. Nefertiti is all over the news. Everybody in the country is talking about her now. She was an equal ruler, a powerful-as-fuck woman, if that doesn't spur on the feminist movement, then I don't know what will.'

'What do you know about feminism?'

'Hey, I'm a staunch feminist. I believe in equal rights for all. Fuck the pay gap.'

'Good answer,' I say.

'And as a proud feminist, I can imagine it's pretty annoying when the majority of people in your career path are men. Offing your rivals and getting your feminist icon more traction seem like good reasons for murder in my book.'

'You're not wrong,' I admit. 'But I still can't see Hermione murdering people. She seems so… normal.'

'It's always the normal ones you have to watch out for,' Dick says, and winks at me. Damn that wink! 'What's that?' He points to the manila envelope on the dining table.

'Rosalind gave it to me earlier, some information about her mum, she said.'

Dick picks it up, without asking. 'It's still sealed.'

'I saw a man die earlier, forgive me if I didn't feel like working today.'

'Prunella is Hermione's sister. Aren't you even a little bit curious about what's inside?'

In the craziness of the day, the connection between Hermione and Prunella hadn't been at the forefront of my mind.

'Pass it here,' I say, holding out my hand for the envelope.

I slice it open and tip the contents onto the coffee table.

'They're letters and a diary,' I say, looking at Dick.

Love Letters

My dearest Penelope,

Since the first moment we met, sharing a well-earned glass of Margaux with the rest of the workers, I knew you were the one. Our eyes met across the room, and all I could see was you. It was like Aten himself shone down only on you. I knew you, of course. Your stellar reputation preceded you. I knew of your husband but prayed that you were estranged. When I saw you holding his hand, and whispering into his ear, I felt my heart break. I didn't know you, but I knew on some intrinsic level that we were meant to be together. That you and I were twin flames – you were the Nefertiti to my Amenhotep. Your name was hot on everybody's tongue – the one who would find Nefertiti. We all have faith in you. You are the reason that everybody is here. You discovered the Amarna amulet when all hope was lost. I have no doubt that you will find our queen's final resting place. You are the reason that we continue to find artefacts daily. You single-handedly continued developing our knowledge and understanding of the ancient ones, but I knew that something else burned deep inside of you. They said you were obsessed with Her. With Queen Nefertiti, and that you wouldn't stop until you found her final resting place. You led us to Sekhemkhet's pyramid, and I saw your frustration when you realised that She wasn't there. We all thought that She would be, but nobody felt your pain quite like I did. Forgive me if this letter upsets you. That is not my aim. I wish to show you that you are a fierce woman, a fierce person, and I admire your steadfastness, your ability to keep striving forward through adversity. With the rumours of rebellion building, will you stay?

Yours forever,
Harold Carson

My dear Penelope,

I am still in shock that you answered my letter. I thought that you would look down upon me as some lowly labourer not fit for your time, and yet you make me feel like I'm the only man on earth. I wish to meet in person, one-on-one. Whenever I am close to you, when we chat and pretend that we don't feel the spark between us, a little bit of me dies. I will do everything I can to support you in your journey. I know that your only priority is finding Nefertiti, and I will be by your side through it all. I heard a rumour that the Egyptian government will soon roll in and take back dig sites by force. Our own governments are advising us to leave this country. They say that we will become a target for the resistance. Our lives are at risk and still you choose to stay. For Her? For me? I will be by your side wherever you go, Penelope. You said that you sent your husband and child away, back to America, and a small part of me prayed that it was for my benefit, not for their safety. You know that we live in dangerous times, and still you refuse to let your dream die. I would die alongside you, Penelope. Meet me tonight and let me say these words to you in person. The place where we first met. I'll bring the wine.

Yours forever,

Harold

Penelope, my darling,

Last night was beyond my wildest dreams. I wish that we could be alone every single night. The rumours of the coup are rife. We will be forced to leave Egypt soon. Shall we leave together? Shall we start a new life, just you and I? We could take your daughter too. Leave your husband and join me, Penelope. I beg you. I am the man you should be with, not him. We both know this. I worship you, just as Nefertiti was worshiped. I would get down on my knees and show you every single day how much you mean to me. You should be treated like the goddess you are. Talk has spread that the Egyptian government will soon come and sweep our archaeological sites, giving us no choice but to leave. Unless we hide. Meet me tonight, and we'll make our plans. No matter what you decide, I will be there.

Yours forever,

Harold

My darling Penelope,

We must lay low until the coup is over. Our site was raided yesterday and many of our staunch supporters were forced to leave the country. I thank our lucky stars that we managed to hide, or else we could have been caught in the skirmish. Ignoring the orders of our own governments, and the Egyptian government, to leave is risky, but it will be worth it. We are so close to finding Her resting place. I can feel it in my bones. We are close. You are close. Stay hidden until things die down, and then we will resume our search. I feel privileged to be with you while you make history. I will meet you in three days, at our usual place. Wear a scarf to cover your hair and face. I will miss you terribly until then. Stay safe, my love.

Yours forever,
Harold

My darling Penny,

I am sorry that our search yesterday yielded no results. I know in my heart that our lost queen is somewhere in the lost city of Amarna. There's nowhere else She could possibly be. We will find her, my love. We will search every single night until She is found. That is my promise to you. Be careful and stay hidden during the day time. Your safety is my priority and I know your mind is focused on other things.

Yours forever,
Harold

Penny,

Last night was the most magical night of my life. You and I, beneath the vast blanket of stars. Never in my wildest dreams did I think it was possible to feel such a way. Everything was perfect. I long to be with you. When all of this is over, and Nefertiti is finally discovered, we will be together. I will meet you tonight at our usual spot. I have a good feeling about our endeavours. Maybe tonight we will find Her. We will make history together, you and I.

Yours forever,

Harold

Penelope,

I am sorry to do this to you. I didn't want us to part in this way, but this is what must happen. I'm not ready to be a father. I didn't mean to give you that impression. I am not meant to be a father. It is not in my blood. Your pregnancy forced my hand. I would have remained by your side until your mission was completed if you hadn't become pregnant. I wish you no harm. I wish you to stay safe. Being a white woman alone in Egypt, especially with child, is a dangerous position to be in. You should leave too. There is nothing for you in Egypt that is worth risking your unborn child for. Nothing, not even Nefertiti, is worth such a risk. You should leave. If you had any sense, you would leave. Go back to your husband and child and live the life a mother should.

Harold

'Wow, Harold's a nob!' Dick says.

I shake my head, trying to find the words to describe how that last letter made me feel.

'Promising her the world and then leaving her when he knocks her up. Classy.' Dick huffs and slams his glass of wine onto the coffee table, it splashes over the rim, but I can't find the strength within me to care. The letters were like reading a love story. Albeit one that centred around cheating, but still… People cheat, it's not unheard of. For this Harold character to change his entire personality after getting Penelope pregnant, it makes me feel sick.

'Who's Penelope?' Dick says.

'Hermione Radcliffe and Prunella Downing's mum,' I explain. 'She was an archaeologist back in the 40s and 50s. She discovered the Amarna amulet.'

'Ah, so that means that one of the sisters is a bastard?' Dick says.

'It would look that way. Although I wouldn't have phrased it like that myself.'

'Which one of them is it?'

'Is what?' I ask.

'The bastard? Which one of them is the kid of this Harold guy, and do you think they know?'

'Rosalind gave me the letters so I would presume at the very least that she and her mum know. Maybe Hermione doesn't. Which one do you think is older, Hermione or Prunella?'

'God, it's hard to tell. Prunella looks like she's had a few nips and tucks, and Hermione seems fairly, *untouched.* Shouldn't be too hard to find out though, should it? For a serious journalist like yourself.'

'It's easy to find out. It's usually somewhere on the internet, and if not, you can search through ancestry sites for their birth certificate.'

'Cool,' Dick says, looking impressed.

'One thing I don't understand though is why Rosalind would want me to see this? This is family gossip, right? The kind that stays within families. Why should she share it with me?'

Dick shrugs, very helpfully.

I can't help but feel like there's something I'm not quite grasping. I recite what we know for sure aloud to Dick, hoping that it will jog my memory. 'So, this Harold Carson was somebody she worked with, and somebody who stayed behind after the Egyptian coup. They continued to search for Nefertiti, even though the government forbade it. They had an affair and Penelope got pregnant. Harold then left her and ran back to the UK.'

Dick nods at me, taking a gulp of his wine. He leans forward so close I think he may kiss me, and says, 'But who is Harold Carson? That's the million-dollar question.'

'Well, that should be easy enough to find out.'

I type the name Harold Carson into Google. As luck would have it, it's not the most popular name. I click on a few social media profiles that show people far too young to be *our* Harold Carson. Time for a new game plan. I type 'Harold Carson + archaeology + Egypt'.

Bingo! There he is. Harold Carson, a young, rugged archaeological assistant. His photograph is included on an archaeology website that outlines the details of different archaeological digs. Egypt – Amarna region – 1949–1952. He looks older than I imagined, but not dramatically so. People back then always looked much older than people do today. There's a thin line of a moustache dusted across his top lip, and he's smiling a quirked smile at the camera. Objectively, he's gorgeous. Old Hollywood, Marlon Brando comes to mind. I take in his photo. Matching his words to his appearance is easy. It isn't difficult to imagine the man in the photo promising a young Penelope the world, and then pulling the rug out from under her. With looks like that, I'd wager he could have gotten away with anything.

I scroll down the page, photos, with captions underneath, show the layout of the digs, the treasures that were found, and also the different people involved in the digs. I immediately spot Penelope Radcliffe and Donald Radcliffe, their appearance familiar to me from the Nefertiti exhibit. They're dotted throughout many photographs on the page, both in the background and included within different groups of people. I scan the page, looking at the photos. I feel the smile grow on my face and don't bother to hold it back. Penelope was clearly a considerable part of the archaeological efforts, she's included in more photos than anybody else. One photo catches my eye. Penelope, sandwiched between her husband and her lover. The date underneath it is June 1952, less than a month before the Egyptian coup. It would stand to figure that it was around that time she sent her husband and daughter to the US for their own safety, and she stayed behind.

Another photo, further down the page, shows Penelope and Donald at the centre, holding up glasses of wine in a 'cheers ' motion. Surrounding them, are other archaeologists and assistants, they're all dressed in the same khaki and sand-coloured clothing. Off to one side, is the young man named as Harold Carson in the initial photo. His glowering face is directed towards Penelope and her husband.

'Somebody looks jealous,' Dick says over my shoulder.

He's right. Harold looks downright livid.

I search his name again with plenty of different additions and find nothing on him. Other than the Egyptian dig, Harold Carson is a ghost.

'So, we need to figure out which one is Harold's kid then,' Dick says.

'That was my next job,' I reply curtly. I know how to do my job.

He holds his hands up in a mock surrender and turns his attention back to the glass of wine in his hand.

Prunella's Instagram is a treasure trove, one that tells me everything I need to know. Prunella posted in May about her 70th birthday. She's silhouetted against a sunset, chin tilted slightly toward the sky like she's soaking in the last of the sun's rays. I'd sell my soul to look half as good as she does at 70.

That means she was born in May 1953, her conception being in 1952. The coup took place in July 1952. Approximately nine months of pregnancy would make the timing perfect.

To confirm, I check Hermione's social media. She's more of a LinkedIn kind of girl. I have to scroll back a few years to get to her 70th birthday congratulatory messages. So, there it is, plain as day. Prunella belongs to Harold Carson and is the result of her mother's affair, while Donald Radcliffe was overseas taking care of Hermione.

'There we go then,' Dick says.

'There we go.'

It feels like a heavy dumbbell has been placed on my chest. This is a lot of information to know.

'Do you really think Prunella knows?'

'She kind of has to, right? If Rosalind gave me these letters, she had to have got them from her mum, surely?'

'I don't know. Families are weird. This one lad I knew, his dad was wanted by the police, and he hightailed it abroad somewhere before he could get caught. It's the family's dirty little secret. Nobody's heard from him since.'

'Rosalind said that this was for my blog post,' I say.

'Her grandmother's illicit affair? Well, it would make for an interesting piece.'

'It would,' I agree. Except for the fact that I won't write about it. This isn't my secret to tell.

Why Me?

'Why me?' is a question I ask myself far too often. I finally convinced Dick that it was time for him to leave. He *did* protest a little. I think there's a small part of him (okay, a big part of him) that wanted round two. I can't let myself go down that rabbit hole. At this point in my life, I need somebody stable, who has their life sorted. Not somebody who works in an off-licence and steals wine. Anyway, when he left, I picked up the diary. A neat A5 leather-bound book with gold-tipped edges. About half the pages within it were fanned open, filled with tiny precise handwriting. The rest of the pages were blank.

I opened it to a random page and began to read.

I've been alone here for too long. I must return home soon, I know that. But how am I to face my husband, my daughter, empty-handed? I promised them Nefertiti, and I have nothing. Well, not exactly nothing. The baby within my stomach isn't yet showing. If I am to pass it off as Donald's, I need to be with him imminently, or he'll suspect something. Another part of me thinks I should just come clean. Donald, more than anybody else, would understand why I allied myself with Harold. I'm not saying that I didn't have fun with him, my lord was it fun, but it was also a means to an end. I needed muscle. I needed somebody to do as I said without asking questions. I needed a person who would keep our secret archaeological efforts to themselves. Some men are more inclined to think with their nether regions than others, and this made Harold the perfect candidate.

But I never expected him to leave when I told him the news. I thought that he'd beg me to be with him. To leave Donald so that we can start a new life together, just as he had before. I planned to let him down easily. I thought he'd been infatuated with me, he'd always behaved as such, which is why it had been so easy to manipulate him into continuing our search for Nefertiti together, but now I see that I was wrong. He'd played me too. But why? What did he get out of it other than a few months of secret trysts? ~~I'm not vain enough to think that it was just about me, and my body.~~ I know that, as a woman, I have significant power over men. I feel a discord in using my femininity, and my body, to get what I wanted from Harold. I have paid the price. This will forever be etched in my mind, a point of contention between my husband and I (whether I choose to tell him or not). I will love the baby regardless, and pray that my husband loves it too, just as much as he loves Hermione. Donald is the best father a child could ask for – I am so lucky to have met him. I only hope that our lives together will not be broken by what I had to do. I did it in the name of Nefertiti. He'll understand. I know he will.

~~If I choose to tell him.~~

~~I should tell him.~~

I won't tell him.

The crossings out are done delicately, a single line through the text. This is a woman at war with herself. I can't imagine how that would feel. It's interesting to note that Penelope was using Harold to support her archaeological efforts. Candour like this would not have been common at that point in time, other than in diaries such as this. A woman using her body to get what she wanted was worse than murder in many circles. Just look at how the world painted the likes of Marilyn Monroe as a whore, just because she wore skimpy outfits. The world is a damn-sight better now, but there's still a long way to go. It's still common to hear people say that a rape victim was 'asking for it' because of the clothes she was wearing. Penelope, a lone woman in Egypt in the 1950s, didn't stand a chance if word got out that she'd used her feminine wiles to convince a man to support her cause. I release a sigh and turn to another page.

I'm on the plane home. My stomach flutters with excitement and trepidation. I cannot wait to see my precious Hermione, and Donald. I am terrified that I will let something slip. I've made the decision to keep the pregnancy a secret. I'm barely two months pregnant by my calculations. It will be easy to feign that the baby came early. For all Donald's intelligence and skill, bless his heart, he doesn't know a thing about pregnancy.

I stare out of the window and watch the bright blue sea beneath us. The white foam as the waves crash together. The endless sky, dotted sporadically with clouds. I feel calmer. The white noise from the plane's engines soothes me.

My life's mission is a bust, so far. I will do all I can from London and from New York, but there's only so much archaeology you can do without being THERE. I think of Nefertiti alone in her slumber, waiting to be found. My heart breaks for her. It breaks for a future where people will not know of her. Her rule is/was radical. She is the very epitome of what it means to be a fearless woman, a leader, a matriarch to rival the patriarchs. If there was ever an image that should represent feminism, it is Nefertiti. I want to raise my children to know that women are of equal value to men, at the very least. Women are not supposed to answer to men, they are supposed to be right there at the forefront alongside them.

While I am returning home now, this isn't the end. I will do everything in my power to return to Egypt and find Nefertiti. I won't rest until then.

I place the diary on my coffee table. None of this makes sense. I get the overwhelming urge to speak to Rosalind and find out why on earth she gave me the letters and the diary. *My mother isn't who she said she is, use these in your write up.* There are thousands of ways I could use this information in my write up of Prunella. Rosalind has to have one specific outcome in mind. She must have expected me to know what she wanted from me. The letters are barely even about Prunella, they're about her mother. The only thing that I can think of is that Rosalind wants the world to know that Prunella isn't Donald Radcliffe's child, but why would that matter? People have been having affairs since the beginning of time, nobody would bat an eyelid at the fact that Prunella's father isn't Donald Radcliffe, but rather her mother's conquest, Harold Carson.

Even then, why me? Why would this information need to come out through me and my article? Prunella has been giving interviews multiple times per month since the beginning of her career, so what makes this one any different?

I catch the time on the clock on my living room wall… 11.47pm. Today has been a nightmare from start to finish. I decide to call it a day and hope that when I wake tomorrow, everything makes sense.

I wake up and everything still makes no sense. It was a fool's dream to hope that everything would click into place while I slept and that I'd know exactly what the universe (and Rosalind) wanted from me when I woke. I need to talk to Rosalind, that much is clear. I have to head to work first, it's *that* day again. *Wake Up & Shake Up.* I slump into the bathroom and see the bags under my eyes. That's what I get for staying up late and drinking too much wine on a work night. I have no one to blame but myself. The shower and the layers of concealer do nothing to hide the dark smudges etched into my face. I shrug, eyeing my make-up warily, it's the best I can do. I head off to work counting down the seconds until it is over and I can get on with what I really want to do… speak to Rosalind, and then delve back into her grandmother's diaries. The Radcliffe/Downing family have clawed their way under my skin. While I'm not sure how useful my new *interest* will be, especially as I'm not going to out Prunella, I can sense a story there. I just need to find it.

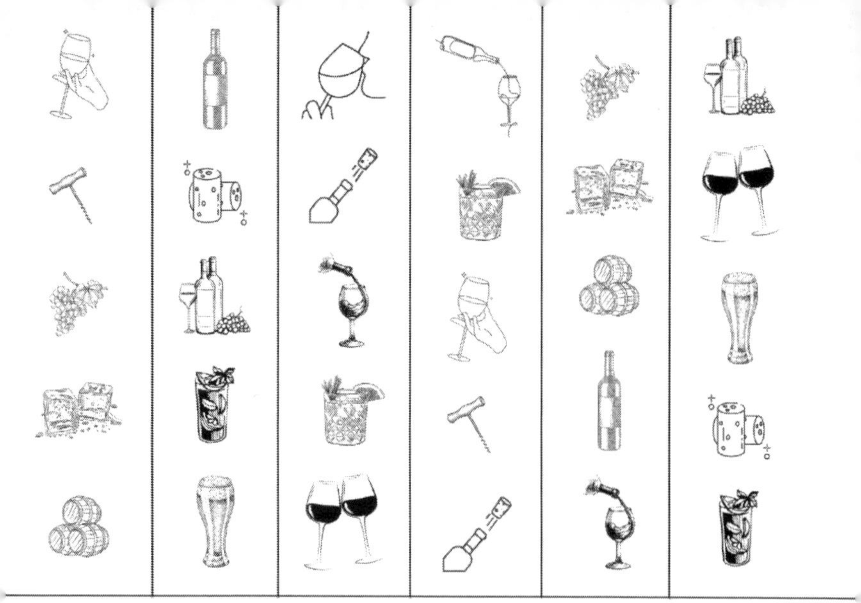

The Truth of the Matter

The theatre where Rosalind is performing in The Merry Wives of Windsor is an unsuspecting building, but I know from experience that it draws a very high-class crowd. It is a theatre for people who *know* theatre. The main double doors that sit next to the box office are closed, but there's a doorway down the alleyway at the side of the theatre. There are always back, or side exits so that the actors can leave without being seen. As luck would have it, the side door is propped open. It doesn't take a detective to deduce from the pile of cigarettes next to the door that this is a popular smoking spot for the theatre staff. I thank the universe for being kind to me and slink inside. Should I be caught, by Prunella or any of the staff, my cover story is simply that I had another couple of questions for Prunella and was passing by the theatre anyway. Hopefully, I won't need the cover story, but it's nice to be prepared.

I head down a corridor that looks like it should lead to the stage. I can hear the rehearsal taking place, voices echo off the tight walls around me. At the end of the corridor is another door, I push it open, saying a silent prayer that it doesn't squeak. The universe is really working in my favour today, and it swings open without so much as a peep. Peering around it, I can see that I'm on the bottom floor of the theatre, to the right of the circle. Rosalind and Prunella are on stage. Prunella is facing off to the left of the stage, delivering a monologue. Rosalind's eyes meet mine and she shakes her head. It's barely perceptible. She holds up two fingers very briefly and then bats at the air with her hand, gesturing for me to shut the door and hide. I retreat, not wanting to get her into trouble.

I decide to make my way back to the alleyway door and wait for Rosalind there.

'What are you doing?' she says. The shuffle of her dress altered me to her before she spoke.

'I wanted to talk to you.'

'So, you came here?' she looks over her shoulder and then back to me.

'Yes. I had no way to contact you.'

She considers my words for a moment. 'Okay. What do you want?'

'I read the letters, but I don't know why you gave them to me.'

'Did you read the diary?'

'Some of it.'

'Look, my mum tries hard. She really does. But she's always had a chip on her shoulder. I found the letters and the diary and read them, and it makes sense. She's always acting. Always. She's obsessed with what people think of her and it's exhausting, for both of us.'

'I don't know what you mean,' I say.

Rosalind gives an exasperated sigh. 'My mum isn't the daughter of a highly respected Egyptologist, historian, and lecturer. She's the daughter of a conman, one who ran out on her before she was even born and has not once tried to find her. She doesn't feel like she belongs. She works twice as hard as everybody else to convince them that she's one of them. If the world found out that she wasn't Grandad Donald's daughter, then she'd know that it isn't a big deal. It would show her that there's nothing to be scared of. The last few months,' Rosalind takes a breath, 'they've been really tough. Things are getting worse. She's constantly attending parties and galas and trying to make out like she's this perfect actor without any faults. She's on her way to a nervous breakdown if you ask me. She doesn't sleep, barely eats. I'm worried about her. I just want her to see that who her father is doesn't matter. Once the world knows, she'll stop trying so hard.'

'What if it has the opposite effect? What if it pushes her over the edge?'

It's obvious that Rosalind cares deeply for her mother. I'm concerned that she's not thought of the aftermath of the letters/diary the whole way through. Yes, it might free her mother from the mental anguish she's feeling, but it also may make it a million times worse.

'I'm desperate. I need to do something. She won't listen to me,' Rosalind says.

I reach out and give her arm a squeeze. 'I know you're trying to do the right thing,' I say. 'I'm just not sure this is it.'

'Please. I'm terrified that she'll spend the rest of her life miserable… or sectioned. I just want her to be happy. I need you to do this for her.'

'I'll think about it,' I say.

'Please. I hope you will.'

'I'm sorry for coming here,' I say. 'Can I have your number, so I don't have to do it again?'

'Sure,' she says. She recites her phone number to me as I add it to my phone.

Rosalind smiles sadly, takes a deep breath, and turns on her heel leaving me alone.

This family! I think.

I leave the theatre still undecided about what I'm going to do. I need to separate myself from Prunella's interview for a while, until I can figure out what I should do. The bottle... That's my distraction.

The bottle is still a puzzle of its own. As far as I can tell, archaeologists genuinely believe that it is a treasure map, or key, to finding some kind of invaluable lost artefact. It strikes me as off, these people, the archaeologists I mean, are all highly educated and yet they believe that a random bottle of wine with some hieroglyphs etched into the surface could help them to find buried treasure. The thought is laughable.

Maybe that's a story.

'Egyptologists Believe Fairy Tale', or something to that effect, would be the working title. It seems a little mean, like I'm poking fun at them, but it is a strange feeling to know that many fully grown and well-educated people would put so much stock in a myth... Hermione included. And then there are the murders of the Egyptologists too. I feel like I'm in an episode of Scooby Doo; treasure maps and murders.

The exhibit is full to the brim when I get there. I called home for the bottle, which is weird, I know. I just don't like leaving something so valuable out of my sight for too long. It takes up most of my satchel, but it's worth it to know that it's there.

Part of me feels bitter about the volume of people at the exhibit. It takes the deaths of three people to draw this kind of a crowd. Nefertiti deserved better than that. I know that Hermione and Penelope would agree with me. I wander around the exhibit, edging around groups of people who are talking loudly and obnoxiously. It's like watching a car crash, I suppose. You can't tear your eyes away. Human beings are weird when it comes to death, it draws them in and refuses to let them go. That's what's happening with the Nefertiti exhibit, either consciously or subconsciously. It makes me feel gross.

I shake the feeling off and force my way to Nefertiti's bust. I stand and look at her face, staring into her eyes. I apologise under my breath for what has happened at her exhibit. This was supposed to be a celebration of the divine feminine energy, not a sideshow circus. I walk around the room, trying not to become too frustrated at the other visitors. Some of them, at least, are genuinely there for the exhibit and they have just as much of a right to be there as I do. I scan the photographs of the insides of various pyramids and tombs. Many of the carvings and paintings that were done directly onto the walls of the pyramids aren't able to be here physically – some were unmoveable, stuck to the structure of the pyramids, while others were too delicate to fly around the world for the sake of a one-off exhibit.

In each depiction of her, Nefertiti stands, or sits, proudly. Her long neck and slim frame seem out of proportion with her head. *This* is what was considered beautiful back then, not some warped social media ideal of what a woman should look like. Beauty standards are always shifting and yet women find themselves slaves to them. I wonder if Nefertiti ever felt like that, or if she was simply wholly comfortable in her skin. It's a weird thought, to consider whether Queen Nefertiti ever felt self-conscious.

I spy Gillian Cox standing next to a relief of Nefertiti. She's talking to a group of older women who are doting on her every word. Gillian Cox is an anomaly amongst the Egyptologists. She doesn't work for an academic establishment. I've Googled her. She completed her PhD, after studying sociology and classical studies, and specialising in Nefertiti, under the tutelage of Hermione Radcliffe. After completing the PhD, she went on to write books on the subject. I downloaded one onto my Kindle. She's a great writer, I have to admit. Although I've barely managed to get past the first few pages given how chaotic my life has been of late.

I wait for her to finish talking to the women before I approach her. I don't want to seem rude, especially not when I'm about to pick her brain. Before I get the chance, Detective Wicks strides up to her, taps her on the shoulder and says something I can't hear. Not wanting to look too conspicuous, but also not wanting to look away, I park myself on a bench and pull out my phone, pretending to doom-scroll. Gillian excuses herself from the group of women and walks away with the detective. They only move a short distance, into one of the corners of the exhibition. I have to angle my body awkwardly to keep an eye on them. The conversation feels tense. The previously smiling Gillian is now stone-faced. She stands silently, her mouth twisted in a way that looks like she's sucking on a lemon and listens to what the detective says to her. She shakes her head. Even from a distance, I can tell that she's holding back what she wants to say. As her face reddens, I consider standing up and saving her from whatever the detective is saying, but then I think better of it. For all I know, Gillian is a suspect, and getting mixed up in a murder investigation is not a wise thing to do. I settle for sitting on the sidelines.

The one-sided conversation, which consists of Detective Wicks monologuing and Gillian (very occasionally) giving one-word answers, lasts only about five minutes. Detective Wicks then nods his head in farewell and leaves. Gillian remains in place. A confused or worried look flashes across her face before she composes herself into an easy smile. Now is my only chance. As much as I don't want to approach her, given that she's experienced something that looked incredibly uncomfortable, I know this is my opportunity. I stand, push my phone into my back pocket (a terrible habit stemming from women's clothing having either no front pockets, or ones that are so shallow you can't fit a cigarette into them, never mind a phone) and make my move.

'Excuse me, Gillian?' I say. I approach slowly, so as not to startle her.

'Oh, hi,' she says.

'I'm Fran,' I say.

'I know who you are, Hermione is a fan of yours.' Gillian smiles kindly at me. She's even more beautiful up close. I almost ask her for make-up tips, nearly forgetting my purpose for being there, before I check myself.

'Is everything okay? I saw the detective...' I leave the sentence hanging, I don't want her to think that I'm prying, but I also do want to know what the detective said to her.

'Yes, he just had some questions about my colleagues,' she says.

'I'm really sorry to hear of their passing,' I say. I never know what to say in the event of people's deaths, but more so when it comes to suspected murder.

'Thank you. Is there something I can help you with?'

'Yes, please,' I say. 'I'm really sorry to bother you, but I did have a question about the bottle of wine that Hermione bought at auction.'

'Oh yeah?' she says, eyeing me suspiciously.

'Yeah. I found it interesting when they mentioned the legend surrounding the bottle at the auction. You know, the fact that it could be a treasure map or something?'

Gillian nods.

'I wondered if you could tell me more about it, for a blog post I'm writing, I mean.'

'What do you want to know?'

'Where did the rumour start?'

Gillian laughs. 'Like all rumours, nobody knows exactly where it started or who started it. There's been talk of this bottle for as long as I can remember. Academics talk about it half-jokingly; the 1943 Grand Vin Du Château Margaux magnum bottle that is said to be the key to lost treasures. Some say it's a map, others say it's a code to decipher. And others think it's a load of shit made up by adults who still want to believe in magic.'

'And what do you think?' I ask.

'Would I like to believe it is real? Sure, of course I would. The thought of finding treasures from the Ancient Egyptians is stuff beyond belief. It would change everything for us.' She pauses and it's like I can see the cogs turning in her brain. 'But, realistically, how could a bottle of wine lead you to lost treasure? This isn't *The Goonies*, real life just doesn't work like that.'

'Thank you.' The bottle weighs heavily on my shoulder.

'Do you know where the bottle is?' Gillian asks, catching me off guard.

'No, I don't,' I reply, too quickly.

'Hmm, okay. Just wondered.' Gillian smiles at me, a crooked smile that makes me suspect she knows my dirty little secret. That the bottle is right in front of her. 'Anyway, I'd better get going.'

'It was lovely to speak to you,' I say.

'You too, Fran.'

I can't help but watch her walk away. The sound of her stilettos clicking on the tiled floor reaches my ears, even above the cacophony of sounds.

While I'm at the exhibition, I decide to have another wander around. Despite the number of people, and the volume at which they're talking, I don't want to part with the Nefertiti exhibit just yet. I find myself standing before Nefertiti's papyrus slippers. It still amazes me that the queen of Egypt wore slippers just like I did. I'd never really stopped to consider what footwear Ancient Egyptian royals would have worn.

The plaque next to the slippers reads:

The Slippers of Queen Nefertiti

Recovered from tomb KV55, alongside many other artefacts from the reign of Akhenaten and Nefertiti. These slippers are made from woven grass and papyrus. It is rare to find such items in such good condition. What makes these slippers most unusual are the markings on their sole, which has been the subject of much contention with archaeologists debating their meaning.

Below the note, is a photograph of the souls of the slippers.

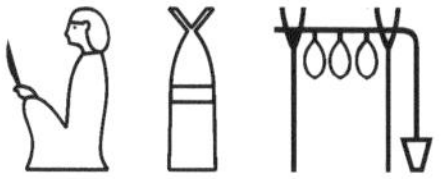

1. Man with knife.
2. Unknown.
3. Grape arbour/wine.

There are no guesses or aspersions as to what the hieroglyphics might mean, or the details of the historical debate. As exciting as Ancient Egypt is (and archaeology in general, I suppose) the uncertainty, and guesswork, would drive me insane. I like facts. Cold hard facts, and historians just seem to make a whole lot of educated guesses.

Something jabs in my mind. Both the bottle of wine, and the slippers, have unknown (and confusing) hieroglyphs on them. I pull out my phone and look at the hieroglyphs from the bottle. As easy as it would be to pull the bottle out of my bag and look at it, it wouldn't be the wisest move.

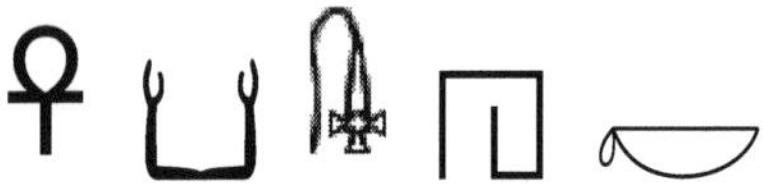

While the bottle's hieroglyphs go from left to right, wrapping around the bottle, the slipper's hieroglyphs run downwards, with *man with knife* at the top and *grape arbour/ wine* at the bottom. I recap the meanings of the bottle's hieroglyphics in my mind.

Treasure, soul, fire, and then initials for a name/place – HC.

I repeat them to myself. *Treasure, soul, fire, H, C.*

Soul.

In researching hieroglyphics, I read that hieroglyphs can be written as homonyms. Two words that sound the same and have different meanings. *Ka – soul. Sole – shoe.* Nefertiti's slipper.

I begin to wonder if I'm going crazy, seeing connections where there aren't any. But it makes sense, in a strange, roundabout way.

I look around for Gillian to ask her if there's a chance the hieroglyphs on the soles of Nefertiti's slippers could have been added *after* they'd been discovered. I don't have the time to think too hard on my suspected nervous breakdown. As I scan the room to find Gillian, the crowd of people begins to move as one, flowing toward Nefertiti's bust. They stand, peering down at the floor, trying to push against one another for a better view.

What's happening? Is something wrong with the bust?

I walk slowly towards the ever-growing group of people and try to see what's happening.

They're all looking at the floor, where Nefertiti's feet would have been if the bust had them.

'What's happening?' I say to a woman standing so close to me that her perfume sticks in my throat.

'A woman's just collapsed.'

'Who?'

'A blonde woman.' Her face screams of exasperation. *How dare I ask questions?*

Gillian.

Could it have happened again? The fourth Egyptologist to be murdered? And the second that I'd witnessed first-hand.

Out of nowhere, as though called by an invisible force (although likely just still hanging around the building after talking to Gillian) Detective Wicks springs into action.

'Move out of the way,' he yells, pushing the gawping crowd out of his way.

As the crowd parts, I see Gillian lying on the floor. Detective Wicks holds a hand to her mouth. She isn't breathing, I presume. He turns his head over her chest, watching for the rise and fall.

'Fuck,' he mutters. The room is in a stunned silence, every single person heard his curse loud and clear. I can't find it in myself to blame him. Even the most professional people have their limits. He's still human. I only now notice that the policemen and security guards have flocked towards Gillian, leaving the exits, presumably, empty.

As though reading my mind, Wicks shouts, 'Nobody can leave the building until we've spoken to you. Please, everybody, stay put for now. We'll try to get round to you as quickly as possible. Now, give me some space.'

Paramedics come into the room with a gurney. They reach down and check Gillian's pulse, shaking their heads. They look to Wicks for instructions.

'Keep her here for now,' he says, and then turns to another police officer. 'Raynor, can you organise for everybody to be taken to the canteen? Make sure nobody leaves.'

'Yes boss,' a younger police officer answers. 'Can everybody follow me please?' he says in a voice that carries well, bouncing off the walls of the exhibition room. He holds his walkie-talkie to his mouth and speaks into that.

Crowd mentality kicks in and people look around at each other before moving. Not one to follow the crowd, metaphorically or otherwise, I'm at the front of the queue following the policeman out of the room. I avoid the temptation to turn around and glance again at Gillian. Only minutes before I'd been speaking with her, and now she is dead.

A phrase enters my head before I can push it away…

Four down, one to go.

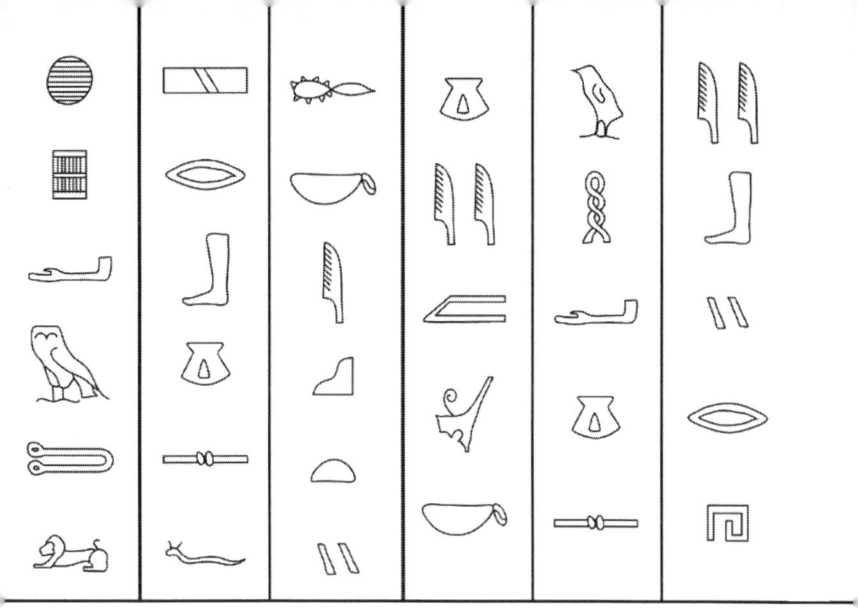

Hermione's Return

Hermione's wail tears at my heart. She walks into the room, accompanied by a policeman. When her eyes settle on Gillian's body, she collapses to her knees and sobs. The whole room of people, currently walking in crocodile formation behind the policeman, stop and stare at her, uncomfortable with the display of emotion. The policeman escorting her looks to his colleague, eyes wide, *what do I do?*

Detective Wicks gestures to the officer leading us out of the room to continue forward.

'Please, ladies and gentlemen,' the officer says, and we do as we're told, following closely behind him.

Hermione remains huddled over her knees, shoulders moving up and down, her whole body shaking. I watch her for as long as I can, a wave of people pushing past me. I resist the urge to go and comfort her. She barely knows me and I don't want to intrude. Detective Wicks, on the other hand, doesn't seem to think twice before walking over to her. He kneels down next to her and places a hand on her shoulders, whispering something into her ear.

'No, no, no,' Hermione repeats over and over. 'This isn't happening. This isn't real.'

A kind paramedic has covered Gillian's body, but it remains in situ.

Hermione makes to stand up and walk towards Gillian, but she is held back by Detective Wicks.

'I'm sorry, I can't let you do that. It's a crime scene,' he says.

I'm forced out of the room by the remaining tide of people.

The canteen looks like a school cafeteria, but slightly more modern. Every single person within the building that isn't police personnel has been cramped into the room. I'm sat at a steel table with three other people, tourists from some European country that I can't quite decipher from their speech. They smiled politely when they sat down, and that's the whole extent of our interaction.

The policeman that led us into the room introduces himself as Detective Raynor. He thanks us for our co-operation and tells us that they'll work as quickly as possible to take our statements and information. I'm keenly aware that Gillian's death is being handled differently than Van Bussell's. Last time, we went into lockdown in the exhibition, but this time we've all been escorted into a different room – staff included – before being locked down. My alarm bells ring telling me that they think the culprit escaped the last time around, and the time before that, and…

There's a solid chance that I'll be here for the long haul, and so I pick up Penelope's diary and flick it open.

The contractions started early this morning. I knew in my bones that she would arrive today. Once more, bittersweet feelings rise to the surface. Since returning from Egypt, I've managed to push the feelings deep within me and lock them away in a box. Thankfully, Donald was so thrilled with the pregnancy news when I told him, that the timeline hasn't come into question. For all he knows, our baby is a couple of months early. Thank goodness for his ignorance. He won't stop buzzing around me today, asking what I need, if there's anything he can do for me. It's sweet but verging on annoying. Our spare bedroom is ready to go, plenty of towels at the ready, and a pair of scissors for the cord. Donald will be there every step of the way, he says. Holding my hand. I'm thankful that we're in London, at least. Should the need arise, the local hospital is only five minutes away, and an ambulance can be here even quicker. That peace of mind will get me through labour, I'm sure. With each contraction, I'm reminded of what I did, what I had to do, the sacrifices I made to find the lost queen. I'm reminded that I failed, and that the consequences will follow me around every day for the rest of my life. Each contraction feels like punishment for my sins.

She's beautiful. Prunella Radcliffe. My darling daughter. I spent hours scouring every detail of her face for glimpses of Harold, but he isn't there, not yet. As of now, I can only see myself in her. I pray that it will remain this way. Hermione is besotted with her sister. She keeps calling Prunella, 'her baby' and then skipping off to play with her toys. I worry about her attention span, but she is only young.

Prunella is feeding from me as I write, my diary is propped on one leg and my writing is crooked. Donald has gone to collect dinner, both of us are exhausted from the labour and in dire need of food. He's taken Hermione with him and now I am alone with my new baby. Our new baby. I have always prayed for daughters. Women are on the cusp of changing the world, soon women will be treated as equals and the world will shift on its axis. New ideas, new perspectives, exciting changes. This is what Prunella (and every other baby girl) represents to the world – a fresh start, the divine power of the female.

I skip ahead a few pages. Penelope's additions are sporadic. She doesn't write every day, or even every week. Occasionally months seem to go by without any instalments. The page I skip ahead to makes me feel like my blood has frozen in my veins.

I saw Harold today. I took Hermione and Prunella shopping – we needed some bits and pieces for dinner. Prunella hasn't been sleeping well and sometimes taking her for a walk in the pram helps to settle her down. Hermione is just happy to be out and about. She's a very easy child, I'm thankful for that. I have a feeling that Prunella is going to be difficult when she reaches Hermione's age. Hermione slept through the night, and then napped multiple times a day when she was Prunella's age. Prunella has an aversion to sleep. They're polar opposites, my daughters.

I was on the high street and decided to pop into the butchers for some meat for dinner. The usual butcher wasn't there, Cutler, his name is. Instead, standing behind the counter bearing a display full of meat, was

Harold Carson. We both stared at each other for a moment before he looked away. I toyed with the idea of walking out of there, but a queue had already formed behind me. I was stuck. I tried to catch his eye multiple times, but he kept looking away from me. It didn't make sense, Harold Carson working in a butchers. While he wasn't a fully-fledged archaeologist, he was a well-practiced archaeological assistant, and had worked on numerous digs. What he lacked in traditional education, he made up for in knowledge. When it was finally my turn, words choked in my neck.

'What are you doing here?' I said.

'I beg your pardon?'

'Harold, what are you doing here?' I asked.

For the first time, I saw his eyes roam to the pram, and the baby within it.

'This is Prunella,' I said. Answering the question, he didn't ask.

'Are you okay, miss?'

'I'm perfectly fine,' I said. 'I asked why you're here.'

'Do I know you?' he said.

'Harold!' My voice raised too high and the people behind me shook their heads and whispered. I paid them no attention.

'My name is Harry,' he said. 'Not Harold. I'm sorry, I don't know you. Now, what can I get for you?'

'Harold, what are you doing?' My face flamed with embarrassment. How dare he pretend not to know me.

'I'm not Harold,' he said. This time, the words were filled with sharp edges. 'I'm Harry. This is my dad's butcher's. What can I get you?'

I had no idea how to react to that. I ran out of the shop with my daughters and went straight home. Prunella woke up just as we left and began screaming her lungs out. She wouldn't settle until we got home. Hermione walked beautifully by my side.

I wanted to scream and cry. I wanted to bang my fists against the walls, but I couldn't. I didn't want to scare my girls. When Donald returned from work, he didn't sense anything was wrong. I wanted to tell him everything then, but I was too deep into the lie. I'd brought this on myself.

I think I'm growing to resent my husband. It's not fair. He doesn't do anything wrong. He's perfect. He works hard, and is loving and kind, but he gets to go out to work every day. He gets to surround himself with history while I have to take care of my children and try to keep them occupied. I'm constantly covered in bodily fluids. I want to be in Donald's place. He'd probably love to take care of the children. He loves being around them. He'd be much better at it than me. He just seems to know what they need. Me? I try my best and it never quite seems good enough. I love my children. I really do, but I need something more. I want to be Penelope Radcliffe, archaeologist, again. Not Penelope Radcliffe, mother. When Prunella gets to one, we'll hire a nanny. Donald is reluctant. He argues that children should be brought up by their parents, which is easy for a man to say. Men's lives don't change all that much after they have children. For women, their whole world changes. They're a mother before all else. I read with every free moment I have. I keep on top of the developments in Egypt. One day, they'll allow me to return. One day, I will find her. Until then, I just have to keep going. I keep my knowledge sharp so that when I am, at last, able to step on the plane and cross the sea, I will be ready. Nefertiti is waiting for me.

A police officer pulls me out of the journal. I look up at him and smile.

'We just need to take your details and a quick statement please,' he says.

I tell him everything, leaving out the details about the bottle I have stashed away in my bag, and then head home. A headache begins to spread across my forehead. Today's been another long and exhausting day. I need a glass of wine, a couple of paracetamol, and I need to speak to Rosalind.

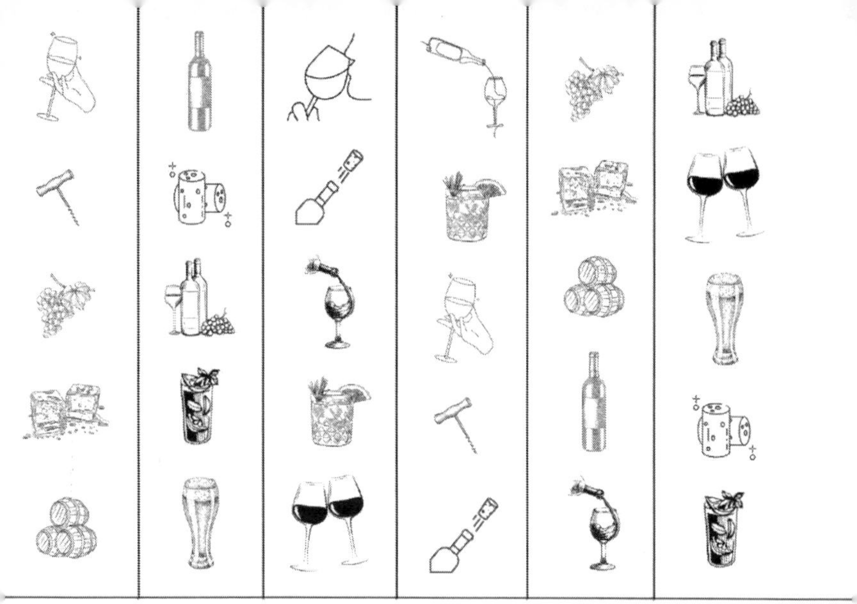

Finally, Some Truth

Hermione's reaction to Gillian's death plays on repeat in my mind. It overrides the image of Gillian's dead body, and Van Bussell's, which had previously taken pride of place in my mind's eye. The noise that came out of Hermione's mouth as she sunk to her knees was the stuff of nightmares. I know that I'll dream of it tonight. There are few noises that hit you quite like a person in that kind of pain. Which leads me to think that Hermione and Gillian weren't just colleagues and friends.

I call Rosalind. She answers on the third ring and says, 'One minute, Sandra.'

I remain quiet until I hear her voice again.

'Sorry about that. Everything okay? Did you make a decision about the article?'

'No, I haven't yet, sorry. I have a couple of questions for you, if that's okay?'

'Go on,' she says.

'Gillian wasn't just Hermione's friend, was she?'

There's a long pause.

'Rosalind?'

'I'm here, sorry.' She sighs. 'No, they weren't just friends. Auntie Hem and Gillian were a couple. They've been together a long time, but neither of them is *out.* You can't say anything…'

'I wouldn't. That's not my place.'

'But you're a journalist,' Rosalind gives a small laugh. 'I thought that journalists didn't have any morals.'

'Some of us do,' I say. When people call me a journalist I still feel like a fraud. I want to say that I'm a *blogger,* but I don't correct them. I smile and take it as a compliment.

'I sensed that,' Rosalind says.

'How come they weren't out?' I ask.

'I don't know. I never asked. I have a few ideas but nothing concrete. They never openly talked about their relationship. They were always *just friends and colleagues* if anybody asked. Which is sad, don't you think?'

'Yeah, it is.' I agree. 'Have you heard from your aunt today?'

'No,' Rosalind says. 'I'm trying to give her some space to grieve. We're not *that* close, you know? I don't know if it's my place.'

'I know you didn't ask for advice, but I would reach out. Even just a text, let her know you're thinking of her. That's all it takes.'

'Yeah, maybe,' Rosalind says. 'Have you finished the journal yet?'

'No, I got stuck at the exhibit while it was locked down.'

'That sucks,' she says.

'Yeah. I'm surprised they don't suspect me yet. I've been there for two of the murders.'

The more I think about it, the more surprised I am that nobody questioned me further, especially after I'd admitted to talking to Gillian right before her death. I freeze, I wonder if mentioning the murders was insensitive for Rosalind.

'You don't seem the type,' Rosalind says.

'No, I suppose not. Sorry to bother you, anyway. Thanks for answering.'

'You're welcome. Goodnight.'

'Goodnight Rosalind,' I say and hang up the phone. There's more to Rosalind than meets the eye. If you saw her on the street, you'd think she was just another Made in Chelsea-esque person, born into money, with not much between the ears, but that couldn't be further from the truth. A reminder to never judge a book by its cover.

As I reach for my glass of wine, there's a knock at the door which never happens because you need a code to get into the building. I heave my body out of my sofa and head to the door.

'Hi,' Dick says, walking through the open door before I can answer him.

'What are you doing here?' I call after him, following him to the living area.

'I was bored. Terry's at work.' He threw himself onto the sofa.

'How did you get into the building?' I ask.

'Your neighbour, Mrs Something-or-other was leaving the building as I got here. She let me in.'

It's easy to translate his words. He charmed her into holding the door for him.

'I expected to hear from you,' he says. 'I heard that Gillian Cox died. I wanted to check that you were okay. You seem very invested in this whole Egyptology thing.'

'I'm okay,' I say. 'I mean, I was there, but…'

'You were there?' Dick says.

'Yeah, I know. Talk about rotten luck.' I try to joke.

'Jesus, that's rough.' He pauses. 'Can I have a glass of that?' He gestures to my glass of wine. I nod and point him in the direction of the bottle. He knows where the glasses are.

'Dick?' I say, watching as he pours a very full glass of wine for himself.

'Yes,' he responds, throwing the now empty bottle of wine into my recycling bin.

'Why are you really here?' I ask.

He nods his head, pursing his lips. 'You're too observant for your own good.' He laughs and takes a long swig of his wine.

'I may feel a little invested in this whole Egypt thing too, okay? You said you were going to look for more clues and if I know anything, it's that you'll have found something.'

'You genuinely think it's going to lead to buried treasure, don't you?' I shake my head and take a sip of my own wine.

'Yeah, I do. My, sorry, our bottle, is at the heart of a great mystery that could lead to a life-changing discovery. I want to be a part of that history. Something to tell the grandkids, you know.'

'You want to split the treasure. Dick, really?!' I can't help but laugh at his explanation.

'If I helped you to find it, you'd kind of have to split it with me, right?'

'Come on! Do you really think that this treasure map will lead to something that will make us rich? It's not a pirate state, Dick. If we find something, and I'm not saying we will, it will likely be of historical value. It won't belong to us. It's not finders-keepers. We're not children.'

'Still... Even if we don't make money from the treasure, there will be TV appearances and interviews, right?'

'And how do you plan to explain your involvement?' I say. 'You're a wine thief who stole the original bottle of wine. You committed a crime.'

'I suppose that's true.' He purses his lips in thought. 'I hadn't thought of that.'

'I didn't think you had. It doesn't matter though, you're getting way ahead of yourself. This isn't TV. This is real life. What are the chances of us actually finding treasure?'

'The scientists believe it though,' he says.

'They're desperate for new artefacts. Maybe they're too close to this.'

'Yeah, maybe you're right. It would be cool to find treasure though. Even if it doesn't make us rich and famous.'

'You're right,' I respond, placating him.

'So, what's new with you?' he asks.

'I think I'm going to write a biographical piece on Penelope Radcliffe,' I say.

'Oh,' Dick says in acknowledgement.

'Yeah, she's such an interesting figure. A lone female archaeologist. A real feminist symbol. Given everything going on at the minute, it could be really good. Maybe it will help me move into more serious journalism.'

'What's wrong with what you do?' Dick asks.

'Nothing, exactly,' I say. 'But have you ever felt stuck? Like you should be doing something more than what you are.'

'Hello! I work in an off-licence and steal expensive wine. Yeah, I think I know how you feel.'

'Fair enough,' I say, batting him on the arm.

'Anything else? Anything, I don't know, bottle related?'

'Yes, actually,' I say. 'Look at this.'

I release my phone from my pocket and show him the photograph of the hieroglyphics on the sole of the slipper.

'Our first hieroglyph included *Ka* which translates to *soul.* Ancient Egyptians often used homophones. It didn't mean soul, like our spirit. It meant sole, like the bottom of a shoe.'

'You bloody genius,' Dick says, smiling from ear to ear.

'So, what do these mean,' he says. 'I presume you've already translated them.'

'Of course,' I say. 'The first one is a man with a knife, I don't know the second, I can't find it, and the third one means wine or arbour, but most likely wine.'

'Man with knife, how, literal…' Dick's laugh is contagious. I can't help but join him.

'Wait, the second one looks like a necklace. If the meanings are literal, could it be a necklace.'

I concentrate on the middle hieroglyph so much that I feel like I'm staring into the Magic Eye books of my youth.

'Hermione,' I whisper.

'What about her?' Dick leans closer to me.

'She wears an amulet that is shaped like that. It's a replica of the Amarna amulet that Penelope Radcliffe discovered in Egypt. It's on display in the Nefertiti exhibit.' I try to slow down my racing brain and think logically about what this might mean. The hieroglyph may not even be of *that amulet* at all, it may just be *an amulet.*

Dick speaks but I shush him, trying to concentrate.

Man with knife.

Amarna amulet.

Wine.

It still doesn't make sense, but it feels like I'm a step closer.

'Let's think step-by-step, okay?' I say to Dick.

He nods eagerly, apparently okay with being my sounding board.

'The first hieroglyph. is a man with a knife but what does that mean?'

He starts to answer but I hold up my hand. I'm speaking my thoughts aloud, not looking for feedback.

'He could be attacking something. He could be making the knife. He could be giving the knife to somebody.'

'Somebody could have given him the knife,' Dick interjects, unhelpfully.

'Okay, and then we have the amulet or necklace.' We both stop to think. It's funny, you can almost see the wheels turning inside Dick's brain. 'Shit, I don't know, I say eventually. I think I need to do some more research on the Amarna amulet. And the last thing we have is the wine or arbour.'

'Could that mean the bottle of wine?' Dick suggests.

'What if the bottle isn't just the first clue, what if it's part of this clue too.'

I'm impressed by Dick's suggestion but try not to show it.

I go to my bag and pull out the bottle. We both stare at it, silently hoping that it reveals its secrets to us. It doesn't. Obviously. It's just a bottle. I feel like I'm on the verge of going crazy.

'I need to go to bed,' I say to Dick when I notice my eyelids getting heavy.

'Okay' he says, jumping off the sofa without hesitation. He walks over to the door. 'See you soon,' he chirps, shutting it behind him.

Once again, I'm alone in my flat pondering the mysteries of Ancient Egypt and how on earth they wound up taking over my life.

A Guilty Obsession

Prunella Downing's interview has been left by the wayside. I can't bring myself to work on it. It's unprofessional as hell, I'm aware, but I've given up trying to concentrate on it. My heart (and my brain, too) isn't in it. My interest in Prunella only goes as far as her link to Hermione and the whole Egyptologist debacle. That's it. Thankfully, I hadn't actually signed any contracts outlining that I would be releasing a blog/article of her interview, so I'm home free. I'm sure she won't even realise.

My entire morning is spent trawling through websites and journal articles that reference Penelope Radcliffe. Just as my printer is about to give up in protest of the sea of pages I've forced it to print, I receive a text from Dick.

I've done something stupid. Can you come and meet me?

My immediate response is to say 'no'. I'm busy and Dick is beginning to feel like a child that I have to take care of, but it's lunchtime and I could do with getting something to eat anyway.

Where are you? I text back.

He responds immediately with, *Starbucks opposite British Museum. Be quick.*

It would kill two birds with one stone; I could see what the hell Dick was moaning about, and I could get a delicious toasty and huge coffee.

Be there soon, I reply.

I grab my things and run out the door. The bottle slips into its usual place inside my bag. I don't like going anywhere without it. It's like a comfort blanket a child might have. I'm scared to leave the house without it. Just in case. *Just in case, what?* I ask myself. The question is futile. I have no idea.

The car journey is quick. I know most people would hop on the tube, but I like to drive. I always have done. Something about subways leaves me feeling claustrophobic. I'll cope with the shitty London traffic, and death stares from environmentalists, if it means I can get around without having to go underground. As I drive, I think about Penelope, and all the other archaeologists out there, particularly those from the early 20th century. I can't imagine what it felt like to traverse the hidden passages of tombs. They likely felt something akin to how I feel on the tube. They can't possibly have known if it was safe, or stable, inside tombs and pyramids. For the first time, I consider how brave archaeologists had to be, especially if they still believed in mummy's curses. You'd never get me in a pyramid, not without a fight anyway.

When I eventually arrive at Starbucks, it takes me a second to spot Dick. He's on a table in the far corner, a baseball cap pulled low over his eyes. There's no coffee in front of him. I hold my hand to my mouth and make a drinking gesture asking him if he wants a drink. He gives a quick nod and I make my way to the tills. I grab two large Americanos and two sandwiches, knowing Dick, he hasn't eaten either.

Once served, I walk carefully to the table with my tray and join Dick.

'Thanks,' he says, pulling one of the bowl-sized mugs off the tray. He drinks deeply from it despite its scalding temperature.

'I wish that was something stronger.' He places the mug back on the table and looks at me. 'If I tell you something, you have to promise you won't call the police. I did it for you,' he says.

'Dick, what did you do?' I ask. I don't intend to make any promises without knowing further details.

'Look,' he says, opening the pocket of his hoodie. I crick my neck awkwardly so that I can see inside his pocket.

'You stole Hermione's necklace?' I ask.

'No,' he says, quietly,

'You didn't,' I say, realisation pouring over me like ice cold water. 'Is that?'

'The Amarna amulet.' His eyes are wide. He clearly regrets his decision.

'Why?' I ask, completely dumbfounded by his actions.

'The hieroglyphics. The treasure. You said you wanted to be a real journalist and do something worthwhile. *This* is worthwhile. The second hieroglyph is the Amarna amulet, I'm sure of it. This is part of the key. We need it.'

'There is no *we* Dick. What the fuck were you thinking?' I keep my voice low so as not to draw attention to us. I needn't worry, the coffee shop is packed to the brim; the lunchtime rush. Nobody is looking at us.

'I wasn't thinking. I was looking at it and one of the members of staff dropped the key for the cabinet It was a snap decision. We needed a break in the case. This is it.'

I'm lost for words. My mouth moves but I can't seem to find a single word to say that would portray the cascade of emotions I'm feeling.

'Nobody knows yet. I thought there would be alarms and stuff, but nobody saw me. I slipped the key into the case, pulled the amulet out, locked it back up and got out of there.'

'Where is the key?' I asked, praying that he hadn't been stupid enough to drop it with his fingerprints all over it.

'Here,' he says, holding open his other pocket.

'Why didn't you run? When they realise it's missing, they'll search the area. You're next door.'

'I didn't think of it like that. I kinda thought I was hiding in plain sight.' He gives me an awkward smile.

'I'm an accomplice,' I say. 'You stole a priceless jewel and told me about it, if I don't tell the police, I'll be an accomplice.'

'I'm going to return it,' Dick says. 'I'm not sure how yet, but once we've solved the treasure hunt, I'll get it back to them. I won't keep it.'

'You'll go to prison. I'll go to prison. This is insane, Dick.' I'm reeling out of control, spiralling at the thought of my whole future going down the drain because of Dick.

'No, you won't. I won't either. I'll figure it out, but for now we have it, and we might as well use it.'

I lose the ability to speak for the second time. The confidence in his voice almost makes me believe that he isn't clinically insane.

'I thought you wanted to be a proper journalist. You said that. This is the chance of a lifetime. If it doesn't lead to the treasure, no harm done.'

'No harm done?' I take a few breaths and try to steady myself.

'Sometimes you have to live on the edge a little, Fran. You always play it so safe. What if this is your chance to make a mark on the world? You've solved more of the mystery than anybody has before. You're making history here.'

The rational part of me wants to throw my coffee in Dick's face for getting me involved in this. That's what I should do. I should tell him where to stuff the amulet and then go and tell the police what I know. But I look into Dick's wide, pleading eyes.

'If you don't return it within the next forty-eight hours, I'm telling the police. Don't make me regret it,' I say, already regretting it the second the words leave my mouth.

'So, what's our next step?' Dick asks. The eagerness reminds me of a golden retriever I had when I was a little girl.

'I don't know yet, Dick. Give me a chance to think, will you?'

He stares at me and waits for me to speak. It's distracting. 'Research. That's what we have to do. You've put a timer on our heads, Dick. We have to solve this thing, and fast, if it's even solvable, which it may well not be. The hieroglyphics have to be the key. I need somewhere quiet so I can think.'

I consider my options. 'The library. At least it will be quiet.'

'Okay,' he says. 'Are you going to eat your sandwich?'

'No, I'm not hungry.' My appetite has vanished without a trace.

'Can I have it?' he asks.

'Fine, whatever,' I say.

'Do me a favour, will you stay a few steps behind me so that I have plausible deniability?'

'Sure thing.'

The library is a five-minute walk away from the Starbucks. One of my favourite things about London is how close everything is. You can find everything you'd ever need within a single square mile. It's brilliant. Very handy when it comes to solving ancient mysteries.

An Unwilling Accomplice

The library smells like home. The familiar scent of old (and new) books wraps around me and I begin to feel myself calming a little. As promised, Dick remains a few feet behind me. Plush sofas surrounding coffee tables are dotted around the open plan main floor. I drop down into one of them and close my eyes. My brain feels like it's vibrating between my ears. I'm an accomplice to a bloody jewellery heist. It seems so insane that I want to laugh. The situation is something that I would never in a million years have envisioned myself being part of. I was strait laced. I *am* strait laced, I just got mixed up in something bizarre, I remind myself. Dick takes a seat on another cluster of sofas.

I hear him sigh loudly like he'd just finished running a marathon. So much for not drawing attention to himself. I shoot him a quick look and he shrugs at me, and winks. I can't think straight with him looking at me. I planned to try and figure out what the hell those hieroglyphs mean. I copy them down into my notepad and stare at them.

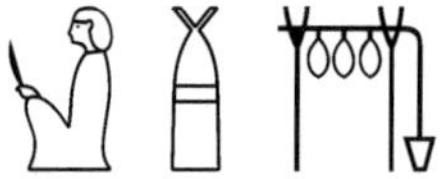

Nothing. They mean nothing to me. I pull up a photograph of the Amarna amulet on my phone and stare at that instead, praying that something will click into place. Dick is right, the amulet looks exactly like the middle hieroglyph. It's a long shot, I'd bet that there are hundreds, if not thousands, of amulets that look exactly like that one. My gut tells me that it does mean the Amarna amulet, but I don't want to be clouded by preconceptions. I go over what I know about the amulet… It was discovered by Penelope Radcliffe in 1952, just before the coup. It is believed to have belonged to Nefertiti due to many artefacts depicting her wearing that exact amulet. Legend has it that it has mind-control powers. I smile a little at the last one, archaeologists seem to love a good myth or legend, which is why the bidding went so high for the wine bottle. The legend attached to it, that it was a map to hidden treasure, made it all the more valuable. A fairy tale for academics.

I stand up, feeling Dick's eyes on my back, I decide to go in search of the Ancient Egypt section of the library. Maybe something there will stand out to me and help me to solve this impossible puzzle. I scan the Dewey Decimal System poster for Ancient Egypt – 932 – and head off in search for it. The section is far bigger than I expected it to be. I scan the titles and wait for something to jump out at me. A few of the books have the word 'hieroglyphic' in the title. I pull them out and squat down on the floor. My first port of call is to flick through the pages and see if anything catches my eye. Out of the five books I pulled off the shelf, two of them seem to focus more on the meaning of specific symbols, a 'key' or cipher of sorts. They're the ones I focus on.

I search for each of the hieroglyphs. As I suspected, the amulet is nowhere to be seen. I find '*man with knife*' with great ease and read the small paragraph underneath the illustration. … *Regularly referring to a cutler or 'knife-maker' and often misinterpreted to mean 'sacrifice'*…

Cutler. Knife-maker. I write next to the hieroglyph in my notepad. I move onto the arbour but find no new information there. The arbour usually refers to wine. The whole thing started with a bottle of wine, so it may just refer to that. However, I write down 'wine bottle?' into my notepad. Maybe it is still useful, or maybe it refers to a different wine bottle. Or, maybe, it refers to something else entirely.

My ringtone echoes around the library.

'Shit,' I mutter, pulling out my phone. Rosalind's name greets me.

'Hello,' I say, accepting the call and putting the phone to my ear.

'Are you free to talk?' Rosalind says.

'Erm, sure,' I reply, glancing back at Dick. He eyes me warily from where he's sitting, but doesn't approach.

'I found something else, I think you should see it.'

'What did you find?' I whisper, afraid to incur the wrath of the stern-looking librarian who'd been sitting at the reception desk when we'd walked in.

'Grandad Donald's diary. I didn't know he'd kept one. Since we'd spoken, I wanted to know what else my mother might be hiding about her past. She'd kept my Grandma Penelope's diaries a secret, so I wondered if there was anything else. Turns out, there was. Can we meet?'

'Now?' I ask. 'I'm in a bit of a situation right now.'

'I can come to you,' she says.

I quickly assess the situation. What harm could come from allowing Rosalind to meet me?

I give her the address of the library and covertly walk back over to Dick.

As I walk by him, I say, 'Rosalind is coming to meet with me here. Can you stay hidden until she's gone?'

Self-preservation had kicked in. The fewer people who saw me with Dick, the better.

'Should I be offended?' he says. Again, he winks at me. All the charm of that wink has rubbed off.

'Yes,' I say. 'Just, stay here please.'

I continue to walk past him and head back to the Ancient Egypt section of the library. I scan my way through various other books but find nothing of note.

Rosalind's perfume causes me to look up from the book in my hand.

'Hello,' I say.

'Thanks for meeting with me. This will be quick, but I thought this would help you.' She hands me a worn spiral reporter's notebook. It is full of jagged handwriting. 'It's my grandad's handwriting. I read the whole thing, but I've left it open on the page I think you'll find useful. Have you given any more thought to your article?'

'I'm probably going to stick with a biography of sorts about Penelope Radcliffe. I think, given everything that's going on right now, people will find it interesting. Your grandmother is a notable figure in archaeology. It's a shame she hasn't had more recognition. From a feminist perspective, at least.'

Rosalind smiles at me. 'She really was ahead of her time,' she agrees. 'But you might want to read this sooner rather than later. It kind of changes things. It's about my mother's real father.' Rosalind pauses and frown lines dance across her smooth forehead. 'I suppose Grandad Donald wasn't really my grandad then.'

I have no idea what to say to that. I can see tears building in her eyes. She blinks them away. 'Sorry about that. I, just, well I feel bad for him.'

'Don't apologise,' I say. 'Thanks for sharing this with me. I'll do Penelope justice, I promise.'

The decision had been made. I couldn't take that promise back no matter how hard I tried. My new, apparently self-funded, project was a biography of sorts about Penelope Radcliffe. Relatively unknown to those outside the field, Penelope's story was both tragic and inspiring. The perfect mix.

'My grandma's obituary is tucked into the pages too. It'll fall out if you shake it.'

'Thank you, Rosalind,' I say.

'No, thank you. I just hope that it snaps my mum out of her bubble before it's too late. Who cares if her dad isn't Donald? So, what if it's somebody who didn't want anything to do with her? It happens all the time. It doesn't mean anything, and it's tearing us apart. I'm just praying that it will make her happy in the long run. She can't go on living like this.'

'Like what?' I ask.

'Her whole world revolves around what other people think of her. She pretends to be something she's not. She's kept this part of her hidden like it's a dirty little secret, like it's something that *she* did wrong. You never know – this might even help her to be proud of her heritage, if your article takes off.'

'I understand,' I say, even though I wasn't entirely convinced I did understand.

'Thank you. I'm sorry to bother you anyway. You're clearly busy.'

'No problem at all,' I say.

I watch Rosalind walk away. Her slumped shoulders are new. Her posture is usually ballerina-perfect, like her mother.

I cast a look at Dick who raises his eyebrows at me in question.

'Later,' I mouth to him.

He shrugs and goes back to staring into space.

I should leave the notepad until later. I'm under a time constraint right now but it weighs heavily on my mind. I shake the reporter's pad and out falls the newspaper snippet of Penelope Radcliffe's obituary. It's small. A typical death notice. Penelope's photograph is about the size of a stamp. Underneath it is her date of birth, and the date of her death.

PENELOPE RADCLIFFE

27th May, 1928 – 6th December, 1972.

Penelope sadly passed away at the age of 44 as the result of injuries sustained in a car accident. She is survived by her husband, Donald, and her daughters Hermione and Prunella. Penelope was a devoted mother and wife. She dedicated her life to raising her children, and to academia. She was a widely known and respected scholar of Egyptology and spent much of the early part of her career in Egypt taking part in archaeological expeditions. She will be deeply missed by family, friends, and colleagues. Her funeral will be held...

A car accident. Until now, it hadn't occurred to me that I didn't know the cause of Penelope's death. If she died in 1972 that meant that Hermione was in her early twenties and Prunella was still a teenager. It must have been incredibly hard to lose their mother at such a young age. It made sense that neither of them had mentioned the way their mother had passed away. The notebook caught my attention. It was open to a page dated 18th December, 1972. The pages folded backwards over the spiral so that this page was all I could see. The page was messy, and the writing looked like that of a doctor, scrawled and barely legible. I squinted to make out the words and began to read.

18th December 1972

Today, my nightmare came true. I buried my wife less than a week ago and the cretinous creature came out of the woodwork today. I'd long since suspected that Penelope had an affair while she was in Egypt. I'd done everything she'd asked of me. I gave up my own career, my own chance at fame, to return home with Hermione and keep her safe. Meanwhile, Penelope had betrayed our marriage. The timeline of the pregnancy never quite clicked with me. Prunella was too big to be as premature as Penelope suggested. I said nothing. Did nothing. My marriage meant more to me than anything in the world, and so I' kept my worries to myself. As Prunella grew I knew I'd been right. Still, I said nothing. I could see myself in Hermione, but not in Prunella.

The knock at the door came when both of my girls were out, thankfully. It took me a minute to place him, as he stood on my doorstep. Harold Carson. The archaeological assistant. At first, I thought he'd just come to give his condolences. And then he opened his mouth.

'Prunella isn't your daughter.' Those were the first words he said.

'I know,' I said.

At first, he looked shocked. He hadn't expected me to say that.

'I need money. A lot of it, or I'm going to tell her she isn't your child.'

I don't remember my exact response, but it was something along the lines of, 'You'd hurt her like that? She's still a child.'

'She's old enough to know the truth. She's, what, seventeen?'

'You'd ruin a girl's life for money?'

'She's a stranger to me.'

'How much?' I said without missing a beat. It wasn't Prunella I was protecting, it was Penelope. I wanted her to remain unsullied in death. She'd hurt me, but she was my wife, my world. I would do all I could to stop Harold from tainting her memory.

'A million,' he said.

'I don't have a million,' I said on instinct.

'Don't be stupid, of course you do. Your wife was the sole heir of the Earl of Cadogan. You have a million pounds.'

He was right. What was Penelope's was now mine. That amount of money was unfathomable.

'You have to leave the country and never come back.'

'Sure, whatever.'

'You said it yourself, I have a lot of money now. If you come back, I will hire a hitman and have you killed.'

I had no idea how the hell I'd follow through on that threat, but if it stopped him from hanging around and asking for more money, then it served its purpose.

'Okay,' he said. The look on his face told me that he believed me, which didn't make any sense to me. I hadn't felt confident in the words I had spoken, but he was content to believe them.

'I'll get the chequebook,' I said. 'Stay there.'

I returned with a chequebook and a pen and began to make out the cheque. As I started to write his name, he held up his hand and said, 'Stop!'

Confused by his outburst I just looked at him.

'Make it out to Harry Cutler.'

'Who's that?'

'Doesn't matter,' he said.

'I need to know who I'm making the cheque to.' My voice was strong and demanding. I have no idea how I made it sound that way when my heart was pounding out of my chest.

'It's me,' he said. His face was turning red, frustration or anger, I didn't know.

'That's not your name,' I said.

'It is. I'm Harry fucking Cutler, not Harold Carson, okay? I lied to get on the dig. Just write the cheque.'

'Fine,' I said. I wrote Harry Cutler as the recipient and filled in the rest of the information. 'Here. If I see you again, I'll have you killed. If you mention the affair to anybody, I'll have you killed. I can do that now. Don't test me.'

'I won't,' he said, sounding like a petulant child. He walked off down the path and I spent the afternoon in my office surrounded by photographs of my wife. I wish she'd told me so that I could tell her I forgave her.

More Than a Knife-Maker

Not only did Harold Carson lie about his name, he was actually Harry Cutler, but he also bribed a widower out of a million pounds. Hardly a stand-up guy by any stretch of the imagination.

'What did she want?' Dick's voice snaps me back to the present.

'Jesus,' I say, spinning around to face him.

'What was that about?'

'You should be over there.' I gesture to the chair I'd left Dick on.

'I know, but then you looked like you'd seen a ghost. And I was bored.' He shrugged like he was being perfectly reasonable.

'You stole a priceless artefact a couple of hours ago. I asked you to keep your distance.'

'Come on, nobody can see us here, between the stacks.' He raises his eyebrows and grins.

'I'm keeping an eye on the news, and it doesn't say anything about the amulet yet anyway.'

'That doesn't mean the police aren't out looking for it, Dick. It just means that it hasn't been leaked to the news. Be sensible.'

'Whatever, just tell me what Rosalind wanted. Terry would be gutted he wasn't here. He still fancies the arse off her, even if she won't see him.'

'She gave me her grandad's diary – Donald Radcliffe.'

'Why?'

'For my article.'

'Elaborate,' Dick prompts. I roll my eyes and he smiles.

'Fine. Harold Carson was actually called Harry Cutler. He conned Donald out of a million pound by threatening to tell the world that Penelope had cheated on him, and that Prunella wasn't his child.'

'He keeps getting better, doesn't he?' Dick shakes his head.

Harry Cutler. Cutler.

'Dick, the company that auctioned the Margaux, what were they called?'

'Cutler and Sons,' Dick says. They're a butchers.'

'Harry Cutler…' I say, and wait to Dick to catch on.

'That has to be a coincidence. There's loads of Cutlers. You don't think that the Cutlers from the butchers are related to Prunella's bio dad?'

'Stranger things have happened. Dick,' I say, a thought snapping at my mind. 'Penelope ran into Harold Carson in a butchers and he pretended not to know her.'

'*That* is weird,' Dick acknowledges.

'I'm going to Google it,' I say.

I type 'Cutler and Sons butchers' into the search engine. The first website that pops up is the right one. It's not the best website. It has the homemade look of many small businesses. At the top of the page is the address of the butchers.

In perhaps the luckiest turn of events, the webpage has a 'meet the team' section. The butchers still seems to be a family affair. The owner is a man called Gordon Cutler. Logic would dictate that he is related to Harry Cutler and will therefore have some information about his whereabouts. Harry Cutler (aka Harold Carson) has not only found himself as a central figure in my research about Penelope, but also in the case of the treasure hunt. A plan forms in my head and I know what I need to do next. Unfortunately for Dick, the plan involves him going home and hiding until everything has blown over. I can't have him following me around as I go to interview Gordon Cutler, not only would it incriminate me if he gets caught, but there's not a single chance that Dick would manage to remain quiet while I talk to the man. As predicted, Dick doesn't take the news well.

'What? I'm just supposed to go home and wait it out? Don't you think the amulet will be central to the treasure map?'

I have no idea at what point Dick decided that the treasure hunt was legit, and I'm not sure when he came to the conclusion that I was the primary treasure hunter in this scenario.

'The hieroglyph says *cutler*. That may just be a coincidence, but if it isn't, then the Cutler's have something to do with this damned treasure hunt. They sold the wine bottle. It makes sense for me to talk to them, okay? I'm going to be much quicker if you're not hanging around.'

Dick looks hurt but nods.

'I'll go home, and I'll hide the amulet. Or maybe you should take it?' he says.

'There's no way on earth I'm taking that amulet with me,' I say. 'I'm already incriminated enough thanks.'

'Can't argue with that. Will you keep me updated?' he says.

'Yeah, sure.' We both know that I'll try to keep my promise, but that there are no guarantees.

'I'm sure the amulet is important,' Dick says, trying to justify his actions, whether to himself or me, I'm not sure.

'You'd better hope so,' I say, wondering if they'll still charge him with the theft if it leads to the discovery of something bigger and better. I hope not. There's no malice in Dick's actions. He's just, well, he's just Dick.

'Go home. I'll call you this evening or sooner if I find anything.'

Dick nods and traipses out of the library, walking like a dog with its tail between its legs.

I hold my breath, do a quick Google search, and wonder how on earth there's nothing about the amulet being stolen from the British Museum. Very strange. Something like that would be front page news, at least for a little while. Unless the police are keeping it under wraps because they think the burglary is connected with the murders. I push that thought way back in my mind. That's the kind of thought that could quickly send a person spiralling.

Google Maps. That's what I need. I type in 'Cutler and Sons Butchers' and it says that the address is half an hour away walking, or almost an hour driving (London traffic!). I decide to walk, not even entertaining the idea of the tube. I walk with purpose and arrive at the butcher's five minutes earlier than predicted. The building is in the centre of a row of shops, the glass-fronted building looks like it was built, or at least refurbished, in the 60s or 70s. It's blocky and grey and, without the huge glass window filled with a fridge of meat, it could pass for a prison.

For a second, my nerves begin to get the better of me. I'm not sure why I'm nervous. It's not like me at all. I take a long, deep, steadying breath and push open the door.

DING DONG. The bell above the door announces my presence.

I'm the only person in the building. The counter takes up the length of the shop. Various cuts of meat look up at me from behind the glass. There's a flap of a plastic curtain and a man in white, with a butcher's cap, walks into the room.

'Hello there, what can I do for you?' he says. The stereotypical cockney accent greets me. It's welcoming, homely.

I chastise myself for not planning what I was going to say ahead of time.

'Are you Gordon Cutler?' I say.

'The one and only,' he says. The smile on his face doesn't quite reach his eyes.

'Do you know Harry Cutler?'

He sighs and pulls the cap off his head, wiping his forehead with his meaty hand. 'I haven't heard that name in a long time.'

'So, you know him?' I say.

'Know him? Yeah, I know him. That's my dad.'

'But you're not in contact with him?' I want to ask if he's alive, but it's a delicate question to ask and I'm not sure how else to broach the subject.

'No. He walked out on me and my mum when I was younger. Haven't seen him since.'

'How long ago was that?' I ask.

He eyes me for a moment too long. 'Who did you say you were?' he says.

'I'm sorry,' I say. 'I'm Francine Witt. I'm a journalist. I'm writing an article about the history of the local area.' The lie came too easily.

He's not sure if he believes me, I can see it in his eyes. He answers me anyway, 'I was 17. He signed this place over to me. Left a note and that's it.'

'I'm sorry about that,' I say. I am sorry, it must have been a difficult thing for a kid to go through.

'He was a bit of a deadbeat anyway. Was never around much before that. It wasn't a great loss.'

'Did you ever look for him?'

'No. He chose to leave. I figured he didn't want to be found when he didn't leave a forwarding address.'

'But why would he leave?' I blurt out.

'You said this was for a project on the history of the local area?' he tilts his head at me.

'Yes, and the establishments.'

'So, you'll be asking everybody about their family drama?'

'I suppose so,' I reply and smile sweetly.

'Fine.' Gordon Cutler purses his lips, thinking. 'I never gave much thought to it if I'm being honest with you. Figured he had another family or something and chose them. It happens all the time.'

'Have you heard of Hermione Radcliffe?' I ask.

'No, should I have?' he says.

'No, I suppose not. She's the lady who won the bottle of wine you auctioned off.'

'Oh,' he says, raising his eyebrows and nodding his head. 'I suppose that's something that my dad did for me. He left that bottle to sell in case of emergencies.'

'He did?' I say, trying to reign in my excitement at a development in the mystery.

'Yeah, in the note he mentioned the wine.'

I barely wait for him to stop speaking before I start. 'What exactly did it say?'

'I don't know exactly. I probably have the note somewhere upstairs still. But he said that the wine was the key to my future and to use it wisely. Or something like that. If you come back in a few days, I can dig it out if it's helpful.'

'I'd really appreciate that,' I say.

'Between the two of us,' he says, 'business is difficult these days so if you're doing a write-up on the local area, that can only be a good thing.'

'That's why you sold the bottle? Because you're struggling?'

'Yeah, people don't shop on the high street anymore. They go to big supermarkets or order online. Means places like this are going out of business left, right and centre.'

I felt a stab of guilt. I did all my shopping online. It was just so easy. I'd not given much thought to the impact it would have on people like Gordon.

'I'm sorry.'

'It is what it is. I'll help with your project as best I can, and I'll make sure the others do. You should know though, Cutlers hasn't always been here. When my grandad had the building, it was over in Bethnal Green. That building wasn't fit for purpose anymore and so we moved here. Our old sign is still above the shop. It would make a great photo for your project.'

I feel terrible. My insides have turned to ice. Gordon Cutler thinks that I'm going to help bring attention to his business when I've used him for my own selfish gain. I'm an awful person.

'Thank you. I'll go and check it out. I'll be in touch soon.'

I hightail it out of there before Gordon can say another word. I take a mental note to follow through on the promise of more exposure for his business. I'm not sure how yet, but I'll figure that out.

A Wild Goose Chase

I'm getting sucked into Dick's delirious dreaming. The wine bottle map. The hieroglyphics. The slipper. The second set of hieroglyphics. Harry Cutler. The whole thing seems like a fever dream. I worry that I'm putting two and two together and getting five. I'm on the precipice of actually believing that the treasure hunt is real, and that it's not just some wild goose chase. It's either real, or a hell of a lot of coincidences. I'm a level-headed kind of gal. I don't get swept up in stuff like this. And yet here I am, making my way to the old Cutler and Sons butcher's because there's a small chance it has something to do with the treasure hunt. I've even texted Dick to bring the bloody amulet, just in case it makes a difference. It was included in the hieroglyphics for a reason, I figure.

The building is ancient. A battered painted sign sits above the door. Blue lettering on a white background. *Cutler and Sons Butcher's Shop*. The windows are thick blown glass, each window is broken down into a four-by-four grid, and each individual pane looks like a drop of water. It's a very sweet old building. The sun is blinding, reflecting from the glass and back into my eyes. I approach the windows and peer inside. There's a layer of dust on the inside of the window that makes it impossible to see anything other than shapes. I have no idea what to do next. If this was Scooby Doo or an Agatha Christie novel, I'd break in and look for clues. This is real life. It's the middle of the day and I'm not one for breaking and entering. I'll leave the criminal activity to Dick for the time being. He's already stolen the amulet, and God only knows how many bottles of wine, what's one more thing to add to his record?

After I text him, Dick arrives in record time. I almost think that he might have been following me, but I decide that's stupid. Dick isn't *that* smart, bless his heart. He looks sweaty, like he might have run the whole way here.

'Did you bring it?' I ask.

'Yes,' he says, about to pull it out of his backpack.

'No, not yet,' I say. 'We need to get into the building.' I'm hoping that he takes the hint. That he volunteers to break into the building.

'We do,' he agrees.

I nod and wait for him to grasp my meaning. We both stare at the building. I sigh and say, 'Any ideas?'

'Funnily enough, breaking and entering isn't one of my many talents,' he replies.

'Surely you can figure it out,' I say.

'Why? Because I'm a thief?' he says.

'Well, yes,' I admit. 'You stole the amulet, you must have some kind of idea how to get into the building without drawing too much attention to us.'

'Let me think. Don't worry, old Dick will figure it out.'

While Dick *figures it out* I study the boarded-up door. The wood used to board it up looks ancient. I reach out and pull the middle one, tentatively, like you would a Jenga block. The rotten wood breaks in my hand.

'That's lucky,' I say. I allow the board to drop to the floor and start on the next one.

'Cover me will you,' I say to Dick. He turns his back to me blocking me from the view of the empty street, just in case. I'm sure it still looks ridiculously suspicious but it's the best I can do.

I pull the second plank away. And the third, dropping them beside my feet. The door behind them looks even more rotten than the boards. Which is lucky, because one push tells me that it's either swollen shut or that it's locked.

'I'm going to have to break it,' I say. Part of me hopes that Dick will be a gentleman and offer to break it in on my behalf. When he doesn't, I kick the door hard adjacent to the lock. I feel it give, which is lucky because I'm not the most physically strong person I know. One more kick and the door swings inwards revealing the dingy room inside. I wish that I'd had the foresight to bring a torch. Despite the light of day, the room inside is murky, dust floats on the air, catching the rays of light and dancing.

'Ready?'

'To trespass? You bet your arse I am,' he says with unwarranted enthusiasm.

'Are you enjoying this?' I turn and ask him.

'Only a little,' he says. Either I'm old, boring, and far too sensible, or Dick is behaving like a child with no concept of the consequences of our actions.

'I'm not sure you should be,' I say.

'Why, this is the most exciting thing to happen to me in years. And, I'm here with a bombshell reporter like you. You really couldn't make this shit up if you tried.' He laughs. I ignore the 'bombshell' comment.

'Can't argue with that. Come on,' I say, and slip inside the building.

Dust lies thick on every surface. Not that there are many surfaces. There's a fireplace, an old dresser, and a threadbare chair.

I pull out the note with the hieroglyphs that I wrote down. Both sets, just in case.

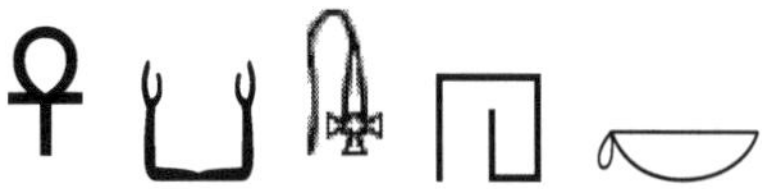

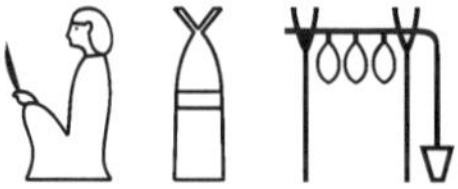

The only one from the first set of hieroglyphs that hasn't come into play yet is the fire. I stare at them against the dimness and wait for something to click. I do the only thing that makes sense to me, and walk toward the fireplace. I pull up the torch on my phone and shine it over the dirty surface. The varnish is peeling off in chunks. It reminds me of my mother's old furniture, varnished one too many times in an attempt to keep it looking new. Using the sleeve of my cardigan I wipe away the grime. It's a fairly standard looking fireplace, nothing fancy. It wouldn't look out of place in any house. It's square in shape with an empty mantelpiece on the top. Maybe at one time it held photographs of the Cutler family. In old buildings, I find it impossible not to think of the ghosts of people who once lived there, or visited. In this case, many of them are likely not still with us. It's a strange thought that would once have tipped me into an existential crisis, but not today. Today, I'm laser-focused on figuring out whether this treasure map has been one big hoax and I've been taken for a fool.

'What are you looking for?' Dick asks. He's wandering aimlessly around the room.

'Clues,' I say.

'So, this is like Scooby Doo! I told you,' he says.

'I don't know. I'd prefer to think it's more Agatha Christie,' I say, not taking my eyes from the fireplace.

'Agatha is far less fun,' he says.

'Precisely,' I reply. 'I don't know about you, but I don't fancy any masked villains showing up while we're digging.'

'Fair enough,' Dick says, laughing to himself.

'See if you can see anything,' I say.

'Like what?'

'I don't know. Anything that looks out of place. The hieroglyphics said *Cutler,* which is where we are. *Amulet* and *wine bottle.* It has to be something to do with the amulet and wine bottle.' I pause. 'If it's anything at all,' I add under my breath.

I listen to Dick's footsteps echoing on the stone floor. My fingertips trace the moulding on the fireplace. They stop when I notice something strange. In the top right-hand corner, the swirling moulded pattern is slightly different from the left.

There's a circle bored into it, about the size of a £1 coin. I go to check the left-hand side and there's no hole. The circle is there but it's only carved a few millimetres deep. I shine my torch once again on the right side. I have a feeling I'm missing something crucial.

I allow my fingers to trail over the area, taking in every carved recess. The numbness in my ankles pulls my attention away and I re-adjust myself, kneeling instead of squatting. From the slightly lower angle, I can see a tiny marking. Not carved. Perhaps burned. The shape of the arbour.

'Did you find something?' Dick says, inches away from my ear.

'Maybe,' I reply, only just resisting the urge to push him away from me.

I pull the wine bottle out of my bag and line it up with the hole in the fireplace. The lip of the bottle is the perfect size to slot in there.

'Woah,' Dick breathes in my ear.

I can feel my heart beating in my temples. If I put the bottle in there and it breaks, I don't know what the repercussions will be. There's no time to second guess my decisions so I push the bottle into the hole. I feel a gentle force fighting against it, but I continue pushing. A mechanical click sounds and grabs the bottle from me, holding it in place. I move my hand away and stare at the bottom of the bottle. Although only an inch of the neck is slotted into the fireplace, it holds steady.

'Guess we know what the bottle's for,' Dick says.

'But nothing happened, there must be something else, a switch or something,' I say. I leave the bottle where it is and move my phone's torch around the rest of the fireplace. I'm missing something, I know I am. There's nothing else on the wood that signifies a switch, a button, or another lock.

'Shit,' I mutter under my breath.

'What makes you think you need to do something else, maybe you turn the bottle like a key.'

Before I can stop him, Dick reaches out and attempts to turn the bottle. It doesn't work.

'Or maybe you push it,' he says, already pushing it.

I see what's about to happen in my mind before it does. Dick pushes the bottle hard and the neck snaps. A loud crack bounces violently off the walls. The rest of the bottle falls. Both of us reach out to catch it.

It hits the floor and shatters. Shards of glass skirt across the stone.

My eyes widen at the emerald green glass pieces. Some the size of my fingernail, others a grain of sand. It's not salvageable.

'What did you do?' I snarl at Dick. My voice quakes in my throat. I feel hot tears of frustration push against my eyes. The pressure is unreal. I repeat myself. 'What did you do?'

Dick doesn't speak. He stumbles over his words. Useless sounds flood out of his mouth.

'Why would you do that? You didn't ask me. You just did it.' My head feels like it's going to explode.

'Why should I ask you? You're not my mother,' he says, joking. *He's actually joking.* He just smashed a priceless artefact, well, not exactly priceless seeing as it sold at auction for a toe-curling amount of money, and he's joking.

'Dick,' I warn.

'Seriously? We're a team. Why shouldn't I have done that? It didn't work. I'm sorry, but that could have just as easily been you.'

'No, it couldn't. I'm not that reckless. I think things through. I behave like a fucking adult, Dick.'

'You wouldn't have got this far if it wasn't for me.' His words are harsh, cold.

'Do you know what, you're right. If it wasn't for you, I wouldn't have even seen the bottle up close. I would have never known about the map. I'm not a thief, Dick. But do you know who would have figured it out? Hermione, because it's her bottle. She would be standing here right now instead of us.'

'Then why didn't you give the bottle back to her when you had a chance? That's on you. Not me. You've been carrying the bottle.'

Dick was right. I could have just given the bottle back to Hermione, but I'd got so swept up in the fantasies, the prospect of finding actual treasure (as much as I didn't let myself believe it), and the murders of the damned Egyptologists, that I hid the bottle. On what? The off chance that I might get a decent story out of it, and it would push me into proper, serious journalism.

'I know why you did it,' Dick says. 'I do. You thought this would be your big break, you'd be taken seriously for once, rather than talking about budget wines. You wanted to be the real deal. The big bad reporter who covers murders and mysteries, and so you kept the bottle for yourself.'

'What's wrong with you?' I ask. The temperature of the room has shifted, as has Dick's attitude. The goofy, somewhat charming, guy has been replaced by something else entirely.

'What's wrong with me? Are you serious?' He waits for me to answer, but I don't. 'Why do you think I'm here?'

I shrug, staring up at him. I want to say *because you've got nothing better to do,* but I think better of it.

'I didn't steal the fucking amulet for nothing. I didn't drop everything and run here for nothing. I make one little mistake and you treat me like shit.'

'You broke the bottle,' I say. 'That's hardly a little mistake. It's a big mistake.'

'It was an empty wine bottle.' Dick blinks like he can't understand why I'm so angry with him.

'That somebody paid a lot of money for. An artefact that could lead to some kind of buried treasure and you broke it.'

'This is real life, Fran. You can't seriously believe that this is real. It's a coincidence that the bottle fitted in there. Everything that's led to this point is a coincidence. Do you really think that an ancient artefact will be in an old butcher's shop?'

I'm confused. Visibly so. Until a couple of minutes ago, Dick was into this. He stole the amulet to help me follow the clues on the bottle, and on Nefertiti's slipper. And now...

'You didn't even realise how much you led me on, did you?'

'Excuse me?' I question, not quite believing the words that came out of his mouth.

'You led me on with your flirting and your tight blouses and the fact that you were always calling and texting me. I stole the amulet for you, and *this* is the thanks I get.'

'I didn't ask you to steal the amulet,' I say. My answer is not enough to explain how I'm truly feeling. I thought I'd made it clear that nothing was going to happen between us, but apparently not.

'Not explicitly,' Dick says.

I can't help myself. I laugh out loud. The sound dies in the air.

'Wow, okay, it's like that is it,' he says.

'Look, I'm sorry if you think I led you on. I thought we were just friends, after that one time, but clearly, there have been crossed wires.'

'I can't believe you,' Dick says. He slowly stands up straight and looks at the floor. 'I thought that we were...'

'It was a one-time thing, Dick. We both agreed on that.'

'Even though I did all this for you?'

I'm not going to get into the same argument again. He stole the amulet on his own accord. He stole the bottle on his own accord. Yes, he sat and listened while I explored ideas and theories, and yes, he always came running if I asked for help, but that's what friends do. My mum always told me that women can't just be friends with men without them expecting something more. Next time, I'll take that advice.

'I don't know what to say.'

'Fuck this,' he says. 'Here, you have this.'

He drops the amulet into my hand from his pocket. The sunlight refracts off it and casts small beams of light around us.

'You can deal with that,' he says. 'I'm done.'

Dick turns on his heel and walks out of the room, leaving me alone with the amulet and the broken bottle.

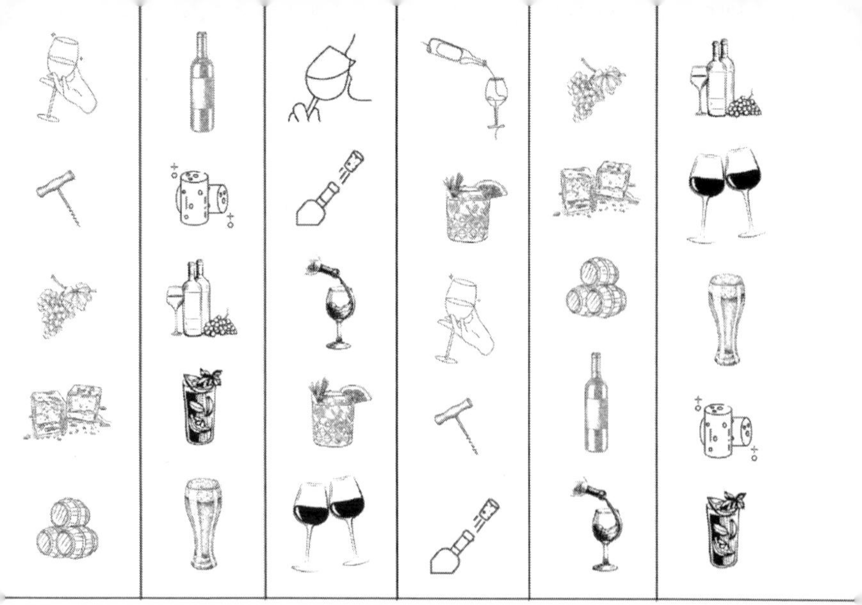

A Dead End

After Dick leaves, the air is still and uncomfortably silent. The amulet sits in my hand. I'm agonisingly aware that I am holding stolen goods, and not just any stolen goods. I dread to think how much the amulet is worth. I need a plan. I need to figure out a way to get it back to the museum without getting into trouble, and preferably without getting Dick into trouble too. I know what he did was wrong, and he behaved like a petulant child, but the thought of Dick getting handcuffed and thrown in the back of a police van doesn't feel good. He's a petty criminal, not a criminal mastermind.

I have two options, as far as I can tell, and that is to continue investigating the old butcher's shop, or to give up and decide what to do with the amulet. I know I have to do something with the amulet eventually, but what's another hour or two?

I return to look at the fireplace using the torch on my phone. There's nothing else on the fire surround or the mantlepiece, I'm certain. I move my attention to the hearth. Two stone slabs a slightly different colour from the rest of the floor, sandier and rougher. And there it is. Where the fire surround connects with the hearth, on the right-hand side at the very bottom, currently dusted with broken glass, is the symbol for the amulet. Ignoring the irritation from the fine shards of glass, I explore the area with my fingers, feeling for anything else. There's a small hole hidden in the recesses of the fireplace, about the size of a thimble. About the size of the amulet.

I feel like my heart will explode out of my mouth. If I slot it in and the amulet breaks, I'm screwed. At best, I'm an accomplice to the theft. At worse, well, I'm not sure, but the best-case scenario still sucks.

I take a deep breath and gently push the amulet into the hole. It fits perfectly.

Nothing happens.

There's no movement. No mechanical click. I pull it back out and try again, pushing a little harder this time. Still nothing. Frustration crawls on my skin like fire ants. I can't believe I thought that would work. My skin burns at my own stupidity.

I pull out the amulet and put it into one of the zip pockets of my bag. I was so certain that I'd figured out the mystery. All signs led to the butchers. Plus, the bottle fitted into the hole in the fireplace. There was even a click that seemed to prove I was right.

Once more, I pull out the note with the hieroglyphs written on it. I cross off each one that has been 'used' to some extent.

I am left with three symbols. Fire, amulet, and arbour. I thought that I'd cracked the code. That the fire symbol meant the fireplace, but maybe it didn't. Maybe I'd wanted it so badly to work that I'd made the symbols fit my own narrative. I sit on the floor, put my head in my hands, and attempt to figure out what the hell I'm going to do next.

I arrived home an hour later, after giving up. The first thing I do is pour myself a glass of wine. A spicy little merlot that I was gifted from a subscription box service in exchange for my 'honest opinion'. I'd neglected my actual job in lieu of a mystery that clearly didn't want to be solved. I throw my bag onto the floor and sink down into the sofa. I'm flooded with so many different emotions. I'm embarrassed, disappointed, exhausted. I sit like that for a long while, trying to decipher how I'm feeling. I can sense the amulet, even though I can't see it in the folds of my bag.

I consider my options:

- Go to the police and tell them everything. *My brain tells me that this is what a 'normal' person would do under the circumstances. Although, I'm not sure anybody decidedly normal would get themselves in this position in the first place.*
- Go to Hermione and explain what happened. *This feels like the safer option. However, Hermione has just lost her partner, and many of her colleagues, I'm not sure I can disturb her at a moment like this.*
- Try to sneak the amulet back into its rightful place in the museum. *I immediately write this off as a bad idea. There's no way I'm capable of that. I don't have a sneaky bone in my body.*
- Go into hiding and try to forget the whole thing happened. *Now, this feels like a good shout. I can go and bury my head in the sand for a few weeks and wait for the whole thing to blow over.*
- Continue to try and crack the code. *There's a niggling part of my brain that, even through the embarrassment, still believes there might be hidden treasure.*

- Cut my losses and pretend the whole thing never happened. *This doesn't take account of the amulet, but it does mean that I can get back to work quickly and attempt to move on with my life. I can continue to write a biographical article on Penelope Radcliffe, and maybe* that *will be my big break.*

There are thousands more options floating around in my brain, but these seem like the only realistic, workable ones. The biggest part of me wants to call Hermione, to ask for her advice. If there was a way I could guarantee that she wouldn't throw me to the police (which I would do in her shoes) then I would. I scroll through the list of contacts in my phone, looking for somebody I can trust, somebody I can talk to about my options, without fear of them phoning the police. For a very brief moment, my eyes settle on Dick's name. No, he showed his true colours. I won't give him the satisfaction. Instead, I dial a different number and Rosalind answers right away.

'Hello,' she says. Her voice sounds sceptical.

'Hi Rosalind. I have a favour to ask you. Are you free?'

'Now?' she asks.

'Yes. It's important. I could really use your help.'

'Is it about my mum?' she says.

'In a roundabout way,' I say. 'Maybe it's more about your aunt.'

She waits for a beat before answering. 'Where shall I meet you?'

I give her my address.

'I'll be there soon,' she says.

While I wait for Rosalind to arrive, I think through my motivation for calling her. Most people would have had a best friend or boyfriend (or a Dick) to call, but I don't have any of those things. Other than calling Keith, my agent, I don't really have many friends. My career has always come first. I'm *that* person who never has time for parties or get-togethers, it doesn't make me particularly popular. Rosalind is arguably my only choice of sounding board at the moment. Weirdly enough, I trust her. I barely know her, but I do trust her.

She arrives less than an hour after I called her, pressing the buzzer on my door and announcing herself. I let her up and wait at the door for her.

'Thank you for coming,' I say. 'Would you like a glass of wine?'

She hesitates before saying, 'Sure.'

I pour her a glass of merlot and we sit on the sofa.

'What is it?' she says.

'I have something to confess,' I admit.

'You said this was about Auntie Hem?'

'Yes. You know her better than I do, and I need your advice.'

'Okay,' she says, leaning away from me.

I tell her almost everything. I tell her about the bottle, the treasure map, the hieroglyphics, the sole of the slipper, Cutler and Sons, and, finally, about how the bottle got broken. I don't mention Dick's name. She sits and listens intently, sipping her wine and looking at me with wide eyes. I tell her about my career, and how I thought that I might be onto something with the treasure maps, and maybe even the Egyptology deaths. I even tell her that I have the amulet. I make it clear that I didn't steal it, but that it did come into my possession. When I'm finished, she says, 'Oh.'

'What do I do?' I ask.

'God, Fran, I have no idea. I don't really know Auntie Hem very well. I do know that she was willing to spend a small fortune on the bottle, so she'll likely be pretty pissed when she finds out it's broken.' She sighs. 'But she's always been a dreamer. Her entire life is Nefertiti and Ancient Egypt. If there's a chance that you're close to finding the hidden treasure, or whatever the hell it actually is, then I think she'll be on board. The amulet, again, I reckon she'll be mad but, I don't know, if there's a chance…'

We sit in silence while Rosalind thinks.

I Google to see if there's anything online about the amulet being stolen. There isn't. Which is weird. Surely it should be all over the news.

'I think we should go and take another look at the butchers. A fresh set of eyes might help.'

I nod, considering her suggestion. 'Sure, I don't see why not. Did you drive here?'

'No, I got the bus,' she says. I raise my eyebrow; she doesn't seem the public transport type. 'I didn't want to phone our driver. I didn't want Mum to know I was meeting you.'

Thankfully, I've only drank half a glass of wine and so I'm good to drive us there, otherwise it would be public transport, and I hate public transport.

'Okay, let's go then.'

'Can I nip to the loo quickly?' Rosalind asks.

'Sure,' I reply, gathering my things together. I grab my bag, the amulet still inside, my phone and keys, and put on a pair of comfy trainers.

'Ready?' Rosalind asks when she emerges from the bathroom.

'As I'll ever be. Actually, one second.' I grab the torch that I keep under the sink in case of emergencies. 'Now I'm ready.'

We ride down the lift to the garage in silence. I'm convinced that Rosalind thinks I'm crazy. She keeps glancing at me with an expression I can't read.

'Thank you for this,' I say as we climb into my car.

'You're welcome,' she says.

We drive on without speaking. When we reach the end of my road, she says, 'It's weird, I kind of feel like I'm dreaming. I can't believe all the stuff you had going on that I didn't know about. Your life is insane.'

'It isn't normally like this. Normally, I go to restaurants and try their wines. I write about the best pinot or the cheapest merlot. I sometimes write about plays and actors. Once a week I go on TV and talk about budget wines. My life is,' I sigh, thinking of the right word, 'comfortable. But it's never like this.'

'It still sounds more fun than mine,' Rosalind says. 'I spend all my time in the theatre, either rehearsing or performing.' She laughs and I chance a quick look at her. 'Do you want to know something funny?'

'Always,' I say.

'I didn't want to be an actor. I don't even like acting. There are thousands of people who would kill to be in my shoes, and I hate it.' Rosalind's attention is turned out of the passenger window.

'Then why do you do it?'

'Because I don't know what I'd do instead. This is all I've ever done.'

'I know that feeling well,' I reply. 'So how did you wind up as an actor if you don't like it?' I know the answer to the question the second the words leave my mouth. *Her mother.*

'It was always expected of me. My mum was a star of the stage, and I grew up in the theatre. I was on stage in Les Mis by the time I was ten. I was young Cosette for Christ's sake. I was really good at it, everybody always told me that. I didn't ever have the option not to do it, I suppose.'

'What would you do instead?'

'I have no idea. It would be nice to go back to university and study something else. Maybe history or archaeology or even journalism. What you do seems fun. I love wine, and I love reading.'

I catch her smiling at the prospect of a fresh start.

'How old are you, Rosalind?' I ask.

'I'm thirty. Mum had me late. Didn't think she could have kids and surprise, here I am.'

'I never gave it much thought, but I always assumed you were a lot younger than me. We're pretty much the same age.'

'Do I seem young?' she asks.

'Yes.'

'I'll take it as a compliment,' she says.

'It is. People always assume I'm a lot older than I am.'

'You do seem like a proper grown-up.' Rosalind laughs. I notice the smattering of freckles across her nose and cheeks.

'I don't feel like one. Especially not today. We're behaving like kids, running around following a treasure map.'

'I'm excited,' Rosalind says. 'This is the most exciting thing to happen to me in years.'

I feel a twinge of sadness at her confession. I hope she's joking.

When we pull up outside the butcher's, Rosalind says, 'Is this it?'

'Uh huh,' I nod.

'Spooky,' she replies. 'Come on, let's go find us some treasure.'

I can't help but laugh as I follow her out of the car and toward the ancient building.

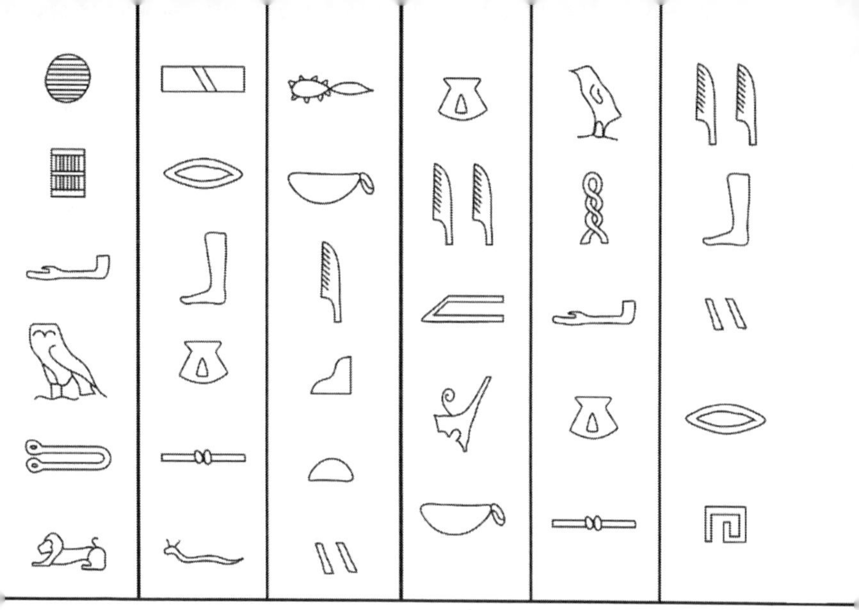

The Element of Surprise

I remove the planks of wood that I'd propped precariously against the door, and we walk inside. In the dim evening light, the room looks like something out of a haunted house. It's unsettling.

'Cool,' Rosalind says. 'What's in the other rooms?'

'Nothing as far as I can tell. They're all empty.'

Rosalind takes the torch from me and walks into the backroom. 'Weird,' I hear her mutter.

'What's weird?'

'There's no fireplace in here.' She's already walking toward the cellar door and down the stairs.

'Why is that weird, I ask?'

'Old buildings like these have fireplaces in every room. It was the only way to keep them warm.'

'Maybe they've been boarded up,' I suggest.

'Maybe,' she says. 'But why would you do that?'

'To give you more flexibility with the floorplan. It was a butcher's shop.'

'There isn't one down here either,' she calls up from the cellar. When she comes back into the front room, she says, 'Can I see the hieroglyphics again?'

I pass her my notebook. 'I crossed some out because they've already been used.'

'Used?' she says.

'Their clues have already led me to something. All that's left are fireplace, amulet, and arbour. thought it might fit into that slot in the fireplace.'

I show her the slot in the fireplace. 'Can I see the amulet?' she says.

I pass it to her, and she does exactly the same thing as I did before.

'Given where the bottle is, it really does look like it should go in here. The hieroglyphs next to each opening can't be random.' Hearing another, relatively sane, person confirm what I'd suspected makes me feel a little easier about my suspected mental decline.

'But it doesn't do anything,' I say.

'No, it doesn't,' Rosalind acquiesces. 'Maybe we should take another look around and see if there are any other hieroglyphs that we're missing?'

'It can't do any harm, I suppose.'

We leave the amulet in place because it seems like that's where it's meant to be. It no longer feels like Scooby Doo, but rather Indiana Jones.

'You take the torch,' Rosalind says. 'I'll use my phone.'

'I think we should be methodical, like a grid search the police use.'

'I agree. Let's start with the cellar and work our way up. That way we can shut it off and forget about it when we're done.'

I nod in agreement, and we head down the cellar steps.

'You take this side and I'll take that?' I suggest. Rosalind starts at the bottom of the stairs, and I walk across the room. We shine our torches up, then down, and then move across a foot and do the same. It won't be a quick job, but at least we'll have done it thoroughly.

The sound of a door slamming upstairs makes me jump out of my skin.

'Who's that?' Rosalind asks.

'I have no idea,' I say. We point our torch to the stairs. A figure stands atop them, slim and petite. The light from the torch picks up the strands of her long fine hair that stray from her usually neat updo.

'Mum?'

Prunella doesn't say anything. She descends the stairs silently in the spotlight of our torches.

'What are you doing here?' Rosalind asks.

'I should ask you the same thing,' Prunella says. Her words are ice.

'I'm…' Rosalind stutters.

'You're helping with *her* investigation,' Prunella says.

'Yes,' Rosalind ventures warily. 'Fran—'

'I know all about what Fran has been doing,' Prunella says.

'What have I been doing?' I interject.

'You've been investigating me, and you,' Prunella glares at her daughter, 'have been tricked into helping her. I noticed my mother's diaries were missing. And Donald's too. Did you really think I wouldn't notice?'

'I'm sorry, Mum, I just thought that if all this came out, then you'd be happier. You wouldn't worry about what people think.' Rosalind takes a step toward Prunella. I want to pull her back. Something about Prunella isn't right. Her usually immaculate make-up is smudged. Her eyes look feral, darting around the room.

'You thought I'd be better off? What are you talking about, you stupid girl?'

'Hey,' I say, holding up a hand. Rosalind visibly shrinks away from her mother.

'You've ruined everything,' Prunella says, crazy eyes fixed on me.

'I haven't even written the article yet. Rosalind was trying to do what was best for you. You don't need to talk to her like that.'

'I wouldn't have to if you hadn't corrupted her.' I don't point out the fact that Rosalind came to me in the first place, it wouldn't be helpful.

'I have no idea what you're talking about,' I say.

'Ironic, don't you think?' Prunella's laugh is cacophonous. It fills the space, too big for the joke she just said.

I look at Rosalind and hope my facial expression conveys my confusion. *What the fuck is happening?* I try to send to her telepathically.

Prunella's laughter stops abruptly, the ensuing silence is deafening. 'Rosalind, I need you to leave.'

'What?' she says.

'Go home. Now. We'll talk later.'

'I don't…' Rosalind says.

'Now.' Rosalind glances quickly at me and then retreats up the stairs, leaving me alone with Prunella.

'How did you know?' Prunella says when Rosalind's footsteps indicate she's left the building.

'Know what?' I genuinely have no idea at all what is happening, a feeling that is becoming far too common in my life as of late.

'Don't act stupid,' she snarls at me. I'm reminded of a rabid dog. 'That I killed them.'

'What?' is the only word I can manage. My head begins to swim and my vision blurs.

'Come on, don't play stupid. You're always at the museum. You're always hanging around my family. The secret meetings with Rosalind, the way you came back to ask me more questions. You're investigating their murders. *You* want to be the one to solve it. To take the glory.' She pauses, giving me the chance to digest what she is saying. 'Were you going to tell the police, or were you going to write about it on your stupid little blog?'

'You murdered them?' I'm not sure whether it's a question or a statement. None of this makes sense.

'Well done,' she says. The smile on her face is haunting.

My instincts are telling me to run but Prunella is blocking the stairs. I know I'm in danger. Prunella thinks I'd figured out that she was the murderer. I hadn't. It hadn't even crossed my mind.

'You think I was investigating the murders?'

'Duh,' she says in an utterly childish way.

A sharp laugh leaves my throat. 'I was investigating a bloody treasure map. I wasn't investigating the murders at all.'

'Do you think I'm stupid? she says.

'Maybe. My God, you've just told me that you're a murderer, and I'm down here trying to find hidden treasure.'

Prunella opens her mouth to speak but nothing comes out at first. When she does speak, she says, 'I don't know what game you're playing but it won't work. Everything was going perfectly until you stuck your nose in.'

'I didn't stick my nose into anything. Prunella, come on, if I thought you were a murderer I'd have gone straight to the police.'

She thinks for a moment. 'Even if you didn't, you were close to figuring it out. It was only a matter of time. You're too close to this.'

She's going to kill me. The realisation slams into my chest and knocks the wind out of me.

'Why did you do it?' I ask. If she plans to kill me anyway, I may as well get some answers. I steady my breathing and put on my bravest face, despite feeling like I'm going to pass out.

'You saw the diaries. You know that Donald wasn't my father. He left everything to Hermione, like it was my fault I wasn't his kid. It was my mother, the slut, she ruined everything. If she hadn't—'

'—You wouldn't have been born.' I feel a strange kinship to Penelope.

'Both of them took everything from me. They ruined my life. Hermione could have shared the inheritance with me, but no. Do you know how much money that was? My mother was practically aristocratic. Hermione could afford to never work a day in her life and I'm stuck sweating in fucking costumes trying to keep my family afloat, trying to keep a roof over our heads.'

'Trying to keep up appearances,' I add.

She shoots daggers at me, but I don't back down.

'So, what if Hermione got the inheritance? You have a good job. You're respected.'

'It's not enough,' Prunella says through gritted teeth. 'I deserve that money. I deserve to not have to worry about how I'm going to make my next mortgage payment, or how I'm going to fix the broken plumbing. Half of that money is mine and she took it from me.'

'So, what, this is all just a ploy to get back at her? You kill her friends, her colleagues, her lover, and what? Does that make you happy?'

A wide Cheshire Cat smile breaks across Prunella's face. 'Oh, you poor stupid girl, I'm going to kill her next.'

It doesn't make sense. None of this makes sense. In the heat of the moment, I feel like I'm trying to cram jigsaw pieces into the wrong places. Nothing fits.

'Why?' I mutter, thoughts still racing through my brain.

'If I just killed her, who would be the first suspect? The sister who was conned out of millions. If I kill her colleagues, she's just the last in a series of deaths. Why would *I* kill the others? I'd never be a suspect. You have to admit, that's pretty smart.'

'It's sick,' I say.

She shrugs and smiles. 'A necessary evil.'

'You're killing her to get back at her for taking your inheritance?'

'I'm killing her to *get* my inheritance. I'm her only family. When she's gone, the money is mine.'

I'm completely lost for words. 'You did all this because of money?'

'I did this because she betrayed me.' Prunella's voice raises with each syllable. 'I asked her for my share, and she refused. She said that it was Dad's money, and he could choose what he wanted to do with it. She wouldn't let me see a penny.' She shakes her head like she's thinking of a particularly funny memory. 'Money makes the world go round.'

'You're insane.'

'I'm insane for doing what's best for my family. I don't want Rosalind to grow up to feel what it's like not being able to make ends meet.'

'You can make ends meet. You're famous. You can live comfortably.'

'Yes, sell my house, downsize, live more frugally. What will people think of me? I have an image to protect. Can you imagine what the gossip rags would say if I moved to the suburbs? The rumour mill would be rife. I couldn't take it. I just couldn't…' Prunella's ruddy face shook, spit flung from her lips as she spoke. 'It's not fair. I did everything right. I went to the right places, schmoozed the right people, took only the most prestigious acting gigs, and it was all for nothing. Hermione stole what I was entitled to. It was my money just as much as it was hers. How could she do that? How could she take that from me?'

'But why now? Donald died years ago.'

'You don't get it. You don't get it.' Prunella mumbles the words to herself like a prayer. 'I knew you wouldn't understand. Nobody does. Even my own daughter doesn't understand me.'

'What don't I understand?' I try to wrangle my voice into something mirroring sympathy.

'Gillian. It's the only serious relationship my sister has ever had. Until she met her, I thought she wasn't interested in relationships. And then Gillian comes onto the scene. They were getting serious, you know? Really serious. It was only a matter of time before Hermione changed her will and left everything to Gillian. I couldn't let her give my money to some whore.' It's almost like she's pleading with me to understand her motives.

'Prunella, you killed all those people based on an assumption that Hermione would give your inheritance to somebody else.'

'It's not an assumption. I know my sister. She's always been backward. Selfish. As soon as I heard about their relationship, I knew it was over for me. I had to act quickly. The exhibition was the perfect opportunity. Two birds one stone. I can take out both Gillian and Hermione, and get my inheritance sooner rather than later.'

'But what if she never left it to you?' My question hangs in the air.

Prunella shakes her head vigorously. 'She did. She did. She did.'

'You can't know that,' I say.

'I do. I do know that!' Prunella stamps her foot like a toddler having a tantrum.

'So, where do we go from here?' I say.

'I kill you. I kill Hermione. I get my inheritance and live out the rest of my years in luxury.'

'Do you really think you're going to get away with it?'

'Yes, I do.'

'Come on Prunella, stop kidding yourself. The police in this day and age have so many resources at their fingertips. There's no way they won't figure out who did it.'

'Well, you see, I thought of everything. The poison that I injected into them all came from Hermione's lab. There's no way somebody like me could have ever gotten my hands on it. They'll either presume it was another archaeologist, or somebody who works at the museum, or they'll think it was a murder-suicide thing. Either way, I'm off the hook.'

I should be thinking tactically, trying to figure a way out of there. 'You can't seriously think that will work? God, you're deluded.' I smile at the absurdity of her thought process. She *actually* thinks she's going to get away with murdering six people.

Prunella returns my smile. Her hand goes to the pocket of her sleek wide-legged trousers. From within their depths, she pulls out a syringe.

'I'm sorry it has to be this way,' she says stepping toward me. 'If you'd just kept your nose out of my business, we wouldn't be here. And including my daughter in this… the audacity.'

'How are you going to explain my death?' I say, desperately grasping at straws. 'If you kill me with that,' I gesture to the needle in her hand, 'they'll link the deaths together. I'm the odd one out. I'm the one that will make them look at other suspects. They'll find you because you killed me.'

'Don't be stupid. You think I don't cover my tracks? I've gotten away with it for this long. What's one more murder?'

Prunella breaks into a run. It happens in a split second and I'm slow to react. She grapples with me, trying to grab my wrists. I flail, trying to remember any self-defence moves from the videos we were made to watch in school in case we're attacked by a man and dragged into an alleyway. I hadn't expected to be using the moves under these circumstances. I can't remember anything from the sodding videos. I see her fist coming towards my head. I duck but it grazes my temple sending stars reeling across my eyes. My vision zooms in and out. I never thought Prunella would be a puncher, I imagined her more as a slap kind of girl. Her fist goes back again, and I raise my hand to block my face. I only notice at the last second that she has the needle firmly in her grasp. I turn and run but she grabs my ankle sending me to the floor. My hands meet the cold stone and slide, scraping at the skin. My knee ruptures in agony, and sparks fly from the joint.

'No!' I hear the scream behind me. The vice-grip-like hand around my ankle vanishes. I turn around, the twist in my knee sends jolts of lightning up my leg.

Prunella is on the floor, Rosalind on top of her. 'No, no, no, no.' Rosalind repeats the word over and over. Her fingers shake as she touches her mum's unblinking face. 'I didn't mean to.' The needle protrudes from Prunella's neck, the plunger pushed all the way in.

'Mum, I didn't.' Rosalind breaks apart at the seams. Her body shakes uncontrollably. She looks like she's having a seizure. She turns back and looks at me. 'She was going to kill you.'

'I know, I know,' I say. I walk over to her and put my hand on her shoulder, attempting to comfort her. I'm alive. Prunella was going to kill me. Instead, Rosalind killed her. It was an accident. Self-defence. That didn't stop the enormity of what I'd just witnessed crush me.

'It's okay. It'll be okay.'

'My mum killed people.' Rosalind looks at me with wide, confused eyes. 'She's a murderer. It doesn't make sense. She can't. She couldn't.'

'You heard what she said?'

Rosalind nods. Her body shakes aggressively. Her feet are bare. She'd only pretended to leave.

'You saved me, Rosalind. You saved me.'

Fake Out

When the adrenaline finally dissipates enough to allow me to control my hands, I phone the police and explain what happened. Rosalind silently sobs beside me. I can't imagine how she feels. The second I hang up the phone, there's a knock at the door. My brain is so foggy that I think, *wow, that's quick.* But, of course, it isn't the police.

'Hello?' Hermione's voice calls out.

'Down here,' Rosalind shouts back.

'How?' I ask.

'I called her at your flat. When I went to the toilet. I thought she deserved to know what we were doing. I'm sorry, I shouldn't have.'

'Don't worry,' I say. 'It doesn't matter right now.'

Hermione blusters down the stairs. 'What happened?' Her eyes widen as she fixes her gaze on Prunella's body. Rosalind looks like she's about to answer. Instead, she collapses into a fit of sobs. Hermione approaches us and reaches out to her, wrapping her in a hug. Rosalind dissolves against her aunt. Hermione looks to me for answers.

'Prunella killed your colleagues. She tried to kill me. Rosalind pushed her out of the way and the, the needle, it…'

'Oh my God,' Hermione breathes. She holds Rosalind tighter. 'Oh honey, I'm so sorry.' She turns and looks at me. 'You called the police?'

I nod.

'Did she say why?'

'I think, maybe, Rosalind should explain.' It seems like a family matter; one I'm already too far involved in for my own good.

'Please,' Rosalind says over her aunt's shoulder.

'Okay,' I say. 'It was the inheritance. She was scared you'd change your will to give everything to Gillian. She killed your colleagues to cover her tracks. She was going to kill you next.'

Hermione blinks in quick succession, like she's trying to make sense of what I've said.

'She did it for the money?'

I nod.

She sighs and pulls back from Rosalind, holding her at arm's length.

'Did you know?' she asks. There's no malice in her voice. Just simple curiosity.

'No. I was worried she was getting more desperate, but I never thought she'd kill somebody.' She said the last two words so quietly that I barely heard them.

'Desperate for what?' Hermione asks.

'She was always so worried about what people thought of her. She'd spend all of her free time obsessing over every little detail of our lives. I told her so many times to get rid of the house, to move somewhere smaller, somewhere we could afford, but she wouldn't. I was worried about how far she'd go.' Rosalind pauses to gather her thoughts. 'But killing people. I can't believe it.'

'People do desperate things in the name of vanity,' Hermione says. 'I never realised she'd gotten this bad. I'm sorry I didn't figure it out sooner. I could have stopped this.'

'You weren't to know,' Rosalind says.

'I should have. She's my sister. I should have known her better than anybody.' Hermione stares down at her sister and sighs deeply. 'Shit,' she says.

'What?'

'The police told me the killer used ricin to poison the victims. It was the reason I was a suspect in the first place. At the uni, we'd been researching Ancient Egyptian medicines for an upcoming exhibit. They used ricin as a laxative, from the Castor

Bean. We'd been trying to mimic their methods for releasing the toxin from the bean. That's how she must have got it.'

'She came to your lab?'

'Yes, a while back. She brought coffee and said she wanted to catch up. I thought she was extending an olive branch. Turns out, she was plotting my murder.'

Sirens wail from the street. Boots stomp across the floorboards.

'We're in the cellar,' I call.

Detective Wicks is the first to walk down the stairs, followed by paramedics and some uniformed officers.

'Ms Radcliffe,' he says, dipping his head.

'Doctor Radcliffe,' she replies curtly.

'I'm going to have to ask you all to wait upstairs,' he says. 'The paramedics will look you over. Don't leave until I've spoken to you all.'

We stand, my knee protesting, and trail upstairs, leaving Prunella behind.

The paramedics check Rosalind and me over. The police placed a lamp in the corner, illuminating the room and so our torches are no longer necessary. Rosalind is completely fine, other than being in shock. I, on the other hand, need to go for an x-ray on my damaged knee. *Just to be safe,* the paramedic says. I promise to go to the hospital after Detective Wicks has spoken to us. A single uniformed officer stands in the corner of the room like a statue while we wait for the detective.

I catch Hermione looking at the fireplace. 'Is that?' she asks.

I nod sheepishly. 'I'm sorry,' I say.

'What happened?'

I tell her everything, just as I told Rosalind only a couple of hours earlier. To her credit, she doesn't look angry or disappointed, she looks intrigued.

'And the amulet didn't work?' she says.

'No, it didn't do anything. The bottle made a click noise, but the amulet didn't.'

'Hmm,' she says. She approaches the hole at the base of the fireplace and removes the amulet. She removes the amulet from her neck and slots it into the hole. There's a mechanical click and a small compartment under where the neck of the bottle sits springs open. 'I have a confession to make. The amulet your friend stole was not the real one. The one I wear is.' Rosalind and I crowd behind Hermione as she opens the compartment fully and pulls out a wooden ring box.

I hold my breath, the air in the room stills.

'Oh my God,' Hermione says.

'What is it?' I ask, leaning over her shoulder.

'Nefer-Neferu-Aten Nefertiti,' she says. 'The Beautiful One Has Come.'

Inside the ring box is a glistening gold signet ring with hieroglyphics etched into the oval bezel. It looks immaculate, brand new.

'It can't be,' Hermione says to herself.

'What is it?' I ask.

'It's her ring. The one in the portraits. It's her ring.'

'Nefertiti's ring?' Rosalind asks.

'Yes,' Hermione says. A smile breaks out across her face. 'I can't believe it. The map was real. It was real! The bottle, it wasn't just a rumour. It was real. You did it, Fran. You actually did it. Do you have any idea what this means? This is the first Nefertiti artefact to have been found for decades. The implications are immense.'

I skirt around Hermione and place my hand into the opening. An envelope, just as I'd suspected. Nobody would go through all the hassle of creating treasure maps without some further explanation. Hermione's eyes grow wider.

'What does it say?' she asks, stepping closer to me.

I peel open the envelope and read the letter.

Gordon,

If you're reading this letter that means you stumbled on hard times. I'm sorry about that, and I'm sorry I'm not there to help you. Hopefully, you were able to follow the clues with relative ease. I'm sure you have many questions. I'll do my best to explain everything here. For a short while, just before you were born, I went by the name of Harold Carson, and I worked as an archaeological assistant in Egypt. I despised the butcher's shop and didn't want anything else to do with it. I wanted bigger and better, and so I lied my way into a job I had no right to do.

At the time, Egypt was a volatile place and UK citizens who worked on digs in the country were banished and so I had to return to England, back to a life that I didn't want to live. I did, however, bring back an insurance policy in the form of a bottle of Margaux (a favourite amongst the archaeologists) and Nefertiti's signet ring, rumoured to have been lost to the world. I found it one evening when working on a dig and slipped it into my pocket. It came back to England in my sock. Nobody needs to know how the ring got here, only that it did. The bottle is your key to success, literally. When I told you that the bottle would change your life, I meant it. The ring is priceless. I carved the hieroglyphics into it before I left. I wrote the hieroglyphics on the bottom of Nefertiti's slipper on the day that we found them too. I formulated this plan over many long hot nights in the Egyptian desert. People will fight over the ring. I can't sell it now because it's too recent. I'll be thrown into jail for theft, but when the time comes, you can sell it. Archaeologists will go crazy for it – they'll pay anything you want. Literally, anything. This will change your life.

I'm sorry I have to leave. I know we've never been close, but I hope this makes up for that.

Love,

Dad

'So, Harold, Harry, whoever he is, stole the ring and the wine and set this whole thing up.' I piece together the puzzle as I speak.

'Seems that way,' Hermione says.

We stand there, waiting for Detective Wicks, and allowing everything to sink in. When I woke up this morning, I didn't for a single second think that I was going to be the victim of an attempted murder. I never expected to witness Prunella die at her daughter's hand. I never expected the treasure map to actually be real. Today doesn't feel real. Things like this don't happen to real people. They happen in Agatha Christie novels and TV dramas. When Detective Wicks enters the room from the basement, looks at the three of us like we're one individual entity.

'I need you all to come back to the station with me. I need to take your statements.'

'Will I be in trouble?' Rosalind's says. Her voice is childlike, and it makes my heart ache for her.

'No. All signs point to self-defence.'

Rosalind breathes a visible sigh of relief.

'Maybe now I'll be able to get some sleep,' Detective Wicks says to the uniformed officer on our way out. For the first time since I became aware of his presence after the death of Professor Abu Hinksley, I see him crack a smile. It's small, but it's definitely there.

I throw myself into bed not caring about the sweat and grime that cake my skin after spending twelve hours in a police station, and another five in A&E. Detective Wicks questioned each one of us individually, which took some time. In order to explain Prunella's actions, I had to relay the whole story from the very beginning. Her self-obsession led her to jump to the wrong conclusion. I had no idea she had anything to do with the deaths. That's the problem when you think you're the main character in everybody else's stories, her paranoia caused her death. If she hadn't tried to kill me, Rosalind wouldn't have had to step in and save me. Prunella would still be alive. She might have even successfully killed Hermione and reclaimed the inheritance she believed she was entitled to.

Every time I close my eyes, I see Prunella's moving face. Her still chest. The needle poking out from her. I want to sleep, but I can't. I try for what feels like an eternity before I give up and sit down on the sofa with my laptop. I start to write the article that will change my life.

Epilogue

I sit down opposite Hermione and Rosalind; a small artfully stickered coffee table eats at the space between us. Hermione chose this coffee shop. It's a trendy boutique place in Shoreditch. It's the first time I've seen either of them since my article was published in *The New Yorker*. I'm still in shock that Keith managed to wangle that, but the subsequent nomination for a Pulitzer prevented me from questioning my literary ability too much. The article, titled 'The Face of Feminism', detailed Penelope Radcliffe's life, her relationship with Nefertiti, and how she paved the way for women in STEM subjects.

'A little birdy tells me that you've been approached to write a memoir about my mother,' Hermione says.

'Yes, that's what I wanted to talk to you about.' In reality, I've been approached by each of the 'Big Five' publishing houses to write the memoir.

'And will you do it?' she asks.

Rosalind smirks up at me from her coffee. She already knows I've accepted the most lucrative offer, and the one that provided me with the most creative freedom. It was important for me to have full creative ownership of the project.

'Yes. I would love to interview you for the project. Your insights would be incomparable.'

'I would be honoured,' Hermione says. 'Do you know what I loved the most about your article?'

'What?' I ask.

'That you showed my mother to be the deeply flawed human she was.'

'Oh,' I say, not sure how to read into the comment.

'I mean it as a compliment, I really do.' Hermione sips her tea and continues, 'There's this misconception that women have to be perfect in order to be inspirational. If you have no flaws, it means you've not lived. You showed my mother to be raw and real and still worthy of praise and reverence. I think that, perhaps, that's where my sister went wrong. She fell into this trap society created, she thought that if she was flawed, she wasn't worthy. If she wasn't perfect, she wasn't worthy.'

Rosalind smiles sadly. 'I told her every day that other people's opinions of her didn't matter. I wish she would have realised that she didn't have to be perfect in order to be loved. I loved her.' A tear rolls down Rosalind's cheek. Despite everything that Prunella had done, she was still Rosalind's mother. A love like that doesn't just go away. Hermione places her hand on Rosalind's and squeezes it.

'Can I ask you something, Hermione?' I say. A question has been playing on my mind since *that* day.

'Anything,' she says, and I think she means it.

'Why didn't you share the inheritance with her?'

'I'm surprised you didn't ask sooner.' Hermione smiles. 'Prunella only asked me for her share of the inheritance once. It was shortly after the estate had been settled and she learned that none of it went to her. My father, Donald, wrote me a letter just as he did to her, explaining his decision to not provide her with an inheritance. I respected my father's wishes.'

'What did the letter say?' I ask.

'I'm paraphrasing here, but in the letter, he explained that Prunella wasn't his biological daughter. He expressed his concern that he'd not been able to love her like a father should because every time he looked at her, he saw the man my mother had cheated on him with. He found it hard to be around her and their relationship dwindled. He regretted this, he said. He said he wishes he'd been a better person, but that he'd never been able to overcome that. He saw that she was growing up to be overly materialistic, greedy, even. He said that somewhere along the way she had lost who she truly was because of her obsession with being something she wasn't. He asked me not to share the inheritance with her because he hoped that she would find happiness in who she truly was, not who she pretended to be. He was scared that the money would enable her.'

'That must have been very difficult for you,' I say.

'It was, to a certain extent, but I agreed with him, and therefore I respected his wishes. If Prunella had told me how much she was struggling, I can't say I would have made the same decision, but she didn't. It was all smoke and mirrors.'

'It's a shame. It didn't have to be like that,' I say.

'I know,' Hermione says. 'I know.'

'I spoke to Detective Wicks earlier, by the way,' I say.

'Oh yeah?' Rosalind says.

'Yes, he said that everything's tied up. Because there's no trial, this whole thing is over. It's done. His final reports are in.'

'What about your friend Dick?' Hermione asks, raising her eyebrows at me.

'What about him?' I say.

'Did he tell you I didn't press charges for him stealing the bottle or the amulet?'

'I haven't spoken to him,' I say. 'But I have received a couple of tips about the wine thieves making a resurgence, so I presume he's fine.'

'And you're not going to write about it for your blog?'

'No,' I say. 'My blog's on an indefinite hiatus at the moment, as are my TV appearances.'

'Because you're a hotshot journalist now?' Rosalind teases.

'Exactly,' I say.

'So, when do you two leave?' Hermione asks.

'October,' Rosalind says.

'I bet you're excited,' Hermione says.

'I can't wait,' Rosalind replies, beaming.

My response is a little more subdued. I'm excited, of course, but I know just how much work there is to be done once we arrive in Egypt. The trip is funded by the publishers and Rosalind is coming as my assistant. She's still figuring out what to do with her life. For the first time ever, her decisions are truly her own. Rosalind is the strongest woman I've ever met, not that she believes me when I tell her this. She half-jokes about how she couldn't even tell her mum that she didn't want to be an actor. I always bite back that the way she's handled herself in the aftermath of her mother's death is admirable. Something as traumatic as that could have broken her. Instead, it has been the making of her. If that's not inspirational, I don't know what is.

Printed in Great Britain
by Amazon

51553499R00143